JUST A VISIT

a Haven Port Island story

DONNA LEE ANDERSON

BLUE FORGE PRESS

Port Orchard, Washington

Just a Visit
Copyright 2019
by Donna Lee Anderson

First eBook Edition August 2021
First Print Edition August 2021

ISBN 978-1-59092-953-7

For information about film, reprint or other subsidiary rights, contact blueforgegroup@gmail.com

Blue Forge Press is the print division of the volunteer-run, federal 501(c)3 nonprofit company, Blue Forge Group, founded in 1989 and dedicated to bringing light to the shadows and voice to the silence. We strive to empower storytellers across all walks of life with our four divisions: Blue Forge Press, Blue Forge Films, Blue Forge Gaming, and Blue Forge Records. Find out more at www.BlueForgeGroup.org

Blue Forge Press
7419 Ebbert Drive Southeast
Port Orchard, Washington 98367
blueforgepress@gmail.com
360-550-2071 ph.txt

*in loving memory of
Donna Lee Anderson*

Just a Visit

a Haven Port Island story

Donna Lee Anderson

CHAPTER 1

Deputy Ethan Mitchell was on duty. He listened, then logged in the call and contacted the Sheriff. This was the procedure he was supposed to follow and he knew the rules.

Ethan liked being a deputy. He liked the steady paycheck, and, although he would deny it, he really liked knowing everything that was going on in Haven Port. His mother said if he wasn't being of service, he would just be called a busy body, but that didn't stop him. He felt information was good to have. You never knew when a tidbit of gossip would come in handy, like that time when Tessa and Floyd had a fight and Tessa sort of accidentally pushed him down the stairs to his death. Deputy Mitchell helped her make sure the 'accidentally' was foremost in the report. He knew that Floyd was a rounder and not afraid to use his fists to make a point, even on his wife. And, there was nothing in the Deputy Handbook that said he shouldn't help her. Ethan took Serve and Protect seriously, especially for those people he liked.

Sheriff Kenneth Owens was at home and, because it was also standard procedure for the on-duty deputy to contact him if they needed to leave the office to answer a call, he wasn't surprised to hear Ethan on the line. Depending on the nature of that call, the Sheriff would just say okay or he himself would go to the scene too. This was a go-to-the-scene call.

When the Sheriff pulled into the vacant lot by the ferry landing, he could see that Ethan had the scared twin boys waiting in his car, ready for interrogation no doubt, and their mother was hovering close by. A fire truck and Aid Car had just arrived and was pulling out equipment. Ethan already had the Crime Scene tape in his hand and was starting to mark-off the area. He was efficient all right.

The Sheriff got out of his car and motioned for the deputy to join him then went to talk to Tom Taylor, the fireman in charge, and to Joe Jordan the paramedic. "Got us a swimmer in trouble or what?"

"Looks like a woman and she's all dressed up. She's on her stomach and we can see a coat and a high heel on one foot." Tom Taylor was giving the report. "We called for a water rescue team. Some divers. This okay with you Sheriff?" The Sheriff and Ethan both nodded assent.

And as if on cue, a pick-up truck with two young men wheeled into the lot. As they got out of the cab the fireman said, "That's the divers. Back in a minute." He left them and walked toward the guys that were already suiting up.

The Sheriff watched as the actions to recover the body got started, then he pulled Ethan aside to tell him they wouldn't need to tape off the water. "But it would be a big help if you'd go into the Ferry office and find out which boat came into the dock on the eleven o'clock ferry run from Seattle. Ethan nodded yes, stifled a salute then gave a stern *don't get out of the car* look at the boys as he walked across the parking lot. He wondered briefly why no tape at this scene then remembered in the Deputy Handbook: *Taping of a crime scene: Public water crimes were only taped off on the land. Water is not controllable.* These might not have been the exact words but that's what it meant.

Inside the small office he saw Terry the ticket gal talking on the phone. "Yeah, it was a woman and the sheriff's here now." She looked up and said, "Gotta go," and she hung up and watched as the Deputy approached with his notebook open, pencil poised, and questions ready.

When the Deputy walked back to the area under investigation, he noted the boys were not in the car, nor were they anywhere to be seen. The sheriff saw him coming and met him at the edge of the lot. "I talked to the boys and we can always talk to them later if we need to. They said you got a statement and they were scared so I sent them home with their mother." "Did you get the info from the office gal?"

This wasn't exactly how Ethan would have handled it, but then, whatever the sheriff said was what it would be. "Yes, I got their statement and one from Terry in the office. I'll get it typed and have the kids sign it."

"That can wait until morning. The kids are pretty upset."

"Okay. What do you want me to do now?" Ethan stood almost at attention waiting for instructions.

The sheriff looked at Ethan. A good man but he

never seemed to anticipate any actions during an investigation.

"Why don't you go back to the office and type up the kid's statement and the ferry report, and I'll be there pretty soon so we can go over it."

"I'm on it," said Ethan and he hurried over to his patrol car, got in and left with lights flashing and siren wailing.

The Sheriff just shook his head and turned back towards the water. He doubted he would ever get the responses from Ethan that he thought were appropriate but you couldn't beat him for willingness and enthusiasm.

The divers were laying the body on the stretcher and as the Sheriff walked over to the gurney he noticed the woman had on only one shoe, one earring, and a dress and coat.

"Hello fellows, thanks for helping out. I'm not sure if you can find anything in the water but would you go back and look at the piling where the body got caught and, well, just look at everything."

These two young men were trained in water search and rescue when it was a boating accident, but this was their first body that just appeared. They waded into the water again. The first one went to the piling in question. A few inches under the water he found the piece of cable that had snagged the coat the body was wearing, and he snipped it off as close to the piling as he could get. His partner was waiting with a container and he slipped it in. Then they both dove and inspected the bottom around the piling but the silt was very thick. They pushed their arms down as far as they could reach and felt around but came up with only an empty glass beer bottle, a full aluminum can of something minus the label, and a bent golf club. No shoe or purse. Not anything that related to the woman.

The sheriff stood watching and when they came from the water he took the container with the snipped off cable and said, "Thanks guys. Don't know what we'd do without you."

He watched the ambulance and fire truck leave then got into his car and headed back to the office. He was making a list in his head. *Call a Deputy to attend the autopsy, get the finger print identification process going,* and *get the statements and reports going.* "Yep," he said out loud. "Things to do."

CHAPTER 2

And... on this same Saturday, but on the later four-thirty ferry another lady visitor arrived too, but by a more conventional way.

Only two days ago a fierce storm came down from Alaska with strong winds and rain mixed with snow. Its havoc was evident everywhere when she and her nephew had boarded the ferry in the small town of Southworth. From the downed trees to the standing water along the roads it certainly looked like winter. However, here on Haven Port Island, it was just cloudy with the sun peeking out occasionally. You could tell it had rained because of the large puddles, but the sadistic stormy weather seemed to have missed this Island.

And if he'd said it once he'd said it ten times, "If you don't like the weather, stick around for a couple of minutes." Then he started talking about that *wonderful place* again. Patricia Rose Olson sat in the back seat and nodded her head yes, but inside she was still screaming *No!* This is not where she wanted to spend her *golden years,* as Willy kept calling them, and especially not in November. She wanted to go home to the warm sunshine in San Diego.

"...and they have bingo and card parties and even trips to Seattle."

Why was he so excited? He wasn't going to live here. He wasn't being stuck in an old folk's home --- with old people.

"The doctor is nice too. I talked to him yesterday and he said he'd be here to meet us. His name's Peter Laferty but they call him Dr. Pete. Isn't that nice?"

She nodded again. *Another doctor to tell me not to eat salt and to drink less,* she thought. *Like I don't already know that drill.*

As they drove off the ferry Pat looked through the window trying to assess just what kind of place this island was. It did look kind of nice with the trees still green and even some stuff growing along the parking lot that looked like purple cabbage and was sort of lacey and pretty.

She shifted in her seat. Breaking her leg and all the deep bruises her hip and body had gotten was not fun, and although she was happy to have the walking cast now, it was still very heavy and this whole ordeal was still such a pain in the neck, and a few other places lower down.

"I'm staying here today, right?" She was still hoping against hope that this was just a visit to check the place out.

"Right. I've made arrangements so that you can stay for at least the time we're in Europe and we leave tomorrow. We went over all this already. Don't you remember?"

Of course she remembered. He was sticking her here while he took his bimbo wife on vacation to Europe.

"... and if you like it here, then maybe you can stay and it would be closer for me to visit. That is of course if you don't cause a fuss like you did at the place in Oregon,"

Oh, yes... the fuss.

It was a little more than a fuss if you asked anyone that lived at the Pleasant Valley Conversant Home, and it wasn't hard for her to do even from a wheel chair. She just waited until everyone was going to the dining room and then she'd started just the littlest fire in the bedpan, put it under the bed and waited until the flame got big enough to set fire to the mattress. Next she removed the bedpan, poured water on the fire and dumped the ashes down the toilet. The only thing left was to wait. Very soon and as expected, a nurse's aid was knocking at her door ready to take her to lunch, but when he opened the door and smoke billowed out of the room he started to yell. "Fire! Fire! Call 911." The rest was pure fun. People running everywhere and residents being wheeled and carried and helped to walk out of the building. Three fire trucks and two paramedic vans later, Pat looked back and was still laughing to herself as she wheeled around the corner and saw the cab she'd ordered waiting for her. No one had been in danger and a little excitement never hurt anyone. Kept the heart working.

They might not have found her during this escape attempt except the cabby had an Aunt recuperating at Pleasant Valley and he recognized her. When she told him she wanted to go to the airport he was suspicious. No luggage, a wheel chair, and she wanted to go where? So, without a word he took her back to check it out and when the director heard about it, well, upset would be a weak description of his reaction.

When Willy asked her about the incident she told him that all she wanted was to be out of there and it seemed like the only solution at the time. After the director of Pleasant Valley asked her to relocate, she'd expected to go home to her own condo in California, but no, the doctors said she couldn't live alone as long as she was on these pain meds and not able to walk alone. She told Willy she didn't need the drugs anymore but he wouldn't listen and so here they were, headed for St. Francis Retirement Home on Haven Port Island, in the Puget Sound across from Seattle. Whoopee!

"And Aunty Pat, we won't have to have any fires here, right?"

She shook her head no. Once you did something like that and people knew, then you didn't repeat it. She wasn't senile yet.

Patricia Rose Olson may have been seventy-one but she was certainly not even close to over-the-hill, and she was as strong as many forty-year olds. Until she had this accident she could run faster than anyone half her age and out-lift most of the women at her gym. All those years of having to pass physicals and being put through the hoops at work to keep her accreditations up-to-dated at the Department of Homeland Security, made her keep to the exercise regime, and really she liked to work out. She was thinking she'd ask this country doctor... this Dr. Pete did he say?... well, she planned to ask him is she could start going to the gym so she didn't lose her upper body strength, that is if this place even had a gym.

And Willy was thinking, *This just might be her*

last hope. And he was also hoping against hope that his Mother's sister would behave. If she didn't, he didn't know what he could do. His wife Bambi suggested a mental institution, but that would be the last straw. He was just sure this place would be right for her, and he was really hoping she would fit in so that she'd want to stay of her own free will.

And Bambi Porter really, really, really hoped Aunty Pat would find St. Francis comfortable too. Will thought that both of the other places had been acceptable and they were at first, but Aunty Pat still found ways to be asked to relocate, and she always complained about the food and the constant supervision of her day. *Like she has something to hide.* It wasn't their fault she broke her leg and got banged up when her Harley crashed, but she'd become their responsibility as her only next of kin, and the one thing Bambi knew for sure was that Aunty Pat would never be living with them. If it didn't work out at St. Francis, well, she'd already checked into the legal angle of committing a person to a mental facility against their will, and the lawyer she'd consulted felt it was very doable with her history of fire setting and the other stuff she'd pulled. Armed with this information Bambi smiled. Now it would be easier to face Aunty Pat if she had to, and feign happiness.

Will and Bambi had only been married for three years and they were still in the honeymoon stage, or so said Bambi's mother. "Make sure you get all the happiness you can because when you reach the seven-year-itch period, you never know what'll happen." And Bambi believed this. Just look at her Mother. Married five times and always the divorce had been at that dreaded seven-year mark. Bambi had already had one experience with this break-up thing in a marriage and wanted to make sure this was not a pattern she would be following too, so she was making an extra effort to insure that Will was *so happy he just wouldn't want to look around,* and this trip to Europe was part of the plan. One whole month of just the two of them exploring and being together every day, all day and all night. No telephones, no talk of business and most of all, no relatives. She smiled every time she thought about all that togetherness. But of course if this plan didn't work out, she would always have the pre-nup he'd signed to fall back on.

CHAPTER 3

William Ivan Porter, Willy to his Aunt Pat and Will to his wife and friends, drove his Mercedes SUV down the exit ramp from the ferry and when traffic made them stop before entering the street, he surveyed the area. Not much storm damage here but there was some activity between the ferry and what looked like an old unused dock. A sheriff's car with lights flashing was parked near the water in the parking lot. Will ignored it but Pat was looking too. She thought, *Could be interesting,* but decided *probably not on this hick island.*

Willy had the directions to their destination memorized. He drove down Willow Avenue and Pat saw St. Mary's Catholic Church and the Haven Port Cemetery as they went by. At the end of the block that held the Mountain View Motel, he turned left onto Lincoln Street but she could see the edge of the Haven Port Golf Course farther down on Willow. Then, in just two short blocks they drove into the parking lot of the

St. Francis Retirement Center.

St. Francis was built in a U shape with two stories. The second floor had a glassed in solarium that ran across the front over the entry. To the right of the main entrance was covered parking for the residents, and on the left was visitor parking but Willy just stopped in front of the entrance and the glass double doors.

He got out and as Willy opened the back door of the car, Pat came sliding out feet first, and before he could get the door fully open she was standing in front of him. Although she was wincing with the pain in her hip and leg, she was smiling at her success.

"I would have helped you. Are you okay?"

"Of course I am, Willy. Just wanted to see if I could do it but I think I'll still need a cane."

Willy just shook his head and got the walker out of the back of the SUV and set it on the ground in front of her. He was still shaking his head when he said, "You still need to use this. A cane will come later. The doctor warned you, remember? Exercise those hip muscles slowly, then use the crutches, then..."

She was all set to say something snarky but she looked at his face and changed her mind. He was only trying to help and she knew she had to learn to accept help until this stupid leg and hip was fit again, so she gave him a half-smile and said, "You're right. I need to slow down and not expect to heal like I did forty years ago."

From inside, Dr. Pete and Sister Nora had watched them drive in and saw the getting-out-of-the-car business.

"What room is she going to be in?" asked Dr. Pete.

"Her nephew picked out the apartment across

from my office. He said she's had some problems with thinking she's strong enough to go for long walks and other things, which he didn't expand on, but he asked if maybe we could keep an eye on her for a few days until she's settled in."

"Maybe she needs more than we offer." Dr. Pete was concerned this would put a burden on Sister Nora since this was not a place that didn't usually offer hands-on medical care and assistance.

"Well, I don't mind seeing to her for a while. We all have periodic times of need and after all, she doesn't know anyone here. She'll probably be a little lonesome and maybe I can help with that."

Dr. Pete smiled at her. "Well, just don't forget we can get the visiting nurse to take the load off you if necessary."

She smiled back. Of course she knew of the service and of course she would use it if it became too much, but she felt that helping new people adjust was just part of her job as the Director of St. Francis Retirement Center.

Sister Nora pushed the button that opened both of the front doors and Willy helped Aunty Pat slowly maneuver the walker into the reception area. Pick up the walker, move it ahead, take a step, move the walker, take a step.

"Dr. Pete?" Willy stepped forward and held out his hand.

"Yes I am. Hello."

"This is my aunt, Pat Olson. Aunty Pat, this is Dr. Pete.

"And this is Sister Nora, our Director," said Dr. Pete. "And you must be William Porter. "Welcome to St. Francis."

Pat looked at them and then chided herself.

Smile, these people are not the enemy, at least not yet. She held out her hand to the man with the grey in his hair and said, "Dr. Pete. Hello." Then offered her hand to Sister Nora.

"We're so glad to see you. Hope the trip wasn't too hard," said Dr. Pete.

"That car is like riding in a fancy bed. I'm just fine." Pat smiled but she was wondering how much longer this would take. She was hungry and, she admitted only to herself, she would really like to take a nap.

Sister Nora smiled and said, "Pat, I'm sure you're tired after that trip from Oregon, so why don't I show you your room and then we can take care of the paperwork after you've rested a bit."

It was like this nun had read her mind.

Dr. Pete turned to Willy. "Stuart will help you bring in the bags and then why don't we all meet in Ms. Olson's room." As he spoke the ladies were already making the slow walk toward the hall and Sister Nora looked back and nodded her head yes.

Stuart came in the door from outside and said, "Ready to unload the car Dr. Pete?"

"Yes. Would you bring the things to A-105?"

"Okay," he said and held the door open for Willy to exit.

Dr. Pete went to find the ladies. The door to the room was still open but he knocked lightly then entered. Pat was already sitting on the bed and Sister Nora was removing her shoes.

"Really, I can do this for myself." Pat wasn't used to being helped with everything, especially taking off clothes.

"I know you probably can, but this is a little welcoming gift from me." Sister Nora finished and took the second pillow from the other side of the bed, fluffed it then laid it on top of the pillow beside Pat. "How about a little lay down until dinner which is an hour away. Then I'll come get you and show you where we eat." As she spoke she was helping Pat lift her legs onto the bed and lay back on the pillows.

Pat was very thankful and that sounded just about right. Rest for an hour then eat, then, well, whatever happened then. "Thank you, Sister."

Willy was outside the door and heard his aunt saying thank you. He was surprised but tried not to show it. He never heard her thank anyone and now she was thanking Sister. Was she starting to soften?

The men set the bags on the living room floor and after he set the computer case on the table Willy started fumbling for his wallet but Stuart just smiled, lifted his hand in a sort of salute and left. *No tipping?*

Willy went into the bedroom. "Now this is nice, isn't it? You should do very well here."

What was it about this kid that irritated her? Then she realized he sounded just like her smarmy sister used to. "I'm fine so you can leave now."

"Okay Aunty Pat. I'll send you cards from Italy and call you as soon as we get home." Then he turned to Dr. Pete. "I think I need to sign something."

The doctor nodded. "Follow me," and led the way back to his office.

Sister Nora looked at Pat. "Are you all set?"

"I'm fine. If I slip off, don't let me sleep through dinner. I'm hungry."

"I could get you something now to tide you over."

"No, I can wait but I just didn't want to sleep through it."

"Don't worry, I won't let you." Sister gently

pulled up a thin wool blanket from the bottom of the bed, laid the door key on the nightstand and adjusted the blinds so the light was dimmer. "Now I'll just go tend to a few things. See you in about an hour."

When the men got to Dr. Pete's office, he indicated the chair for Willy and said, "Would you like a cup of coffee?" He made a motion towards the coffee pot he kept behind his desk.

"That would be good. A little sugar too, please."

Dr. Pete poured the coffee and put the cup and the sugar container on the desk in front of Willy. Then he put a spoon and a napkin beside that. "Anything special I need to know that's not in your aunt's folder?"

"I don't think so. Her medical record was sent here, wasn't it? So you know about the leg and hip and ribs and how much she was bruised and generally smashed up. I guess I need to tell you too that she can be a difficult patient because she thinks she's still thirty and will be up and running again in a few days. And I mean running."

Dr. Pete smiled. He knew about these kinds of patients.

Sister Nora entered and laid papers in front of Dr. Pete and then she quietly left the room.

"Let me look." Dr. Pete opened the folder. The medical report and the supporting documents showed the upper left leg had been bruised and tendons and ligaments involved too. The lower right leg had a tibia broken in two places and a cracked fibula with torn muscles. The surgeon had placed screws to hold the bone in place and the most recent x-ray showed those bones were knitting as expected. There had been two operations and unless complications present themselves, no more were planned. Notes from the surgeon mentioned her *faster than expected recovery for a patient of this age,* and a side note said *the patient pushes herself too fast and expects too much, too soon.*

The report also told about the badly bruised right hip and the bruised ribs on the right side along with the bruised right arm. "Do I understand your aunt is seventy-two and she was in a motorcycle accident?"

"You do understand it right." Will sighed. "She was riding her Harley Sportster on the freeway and a big piece of wood fell off a truck. She avoided that but when the car in the next lane swerved to avoid it too, he hit the rear-end of her bike and drove her off the road. I think she's lucky to only have those bruised ribs and the broken leg. Thank God she was wearing a good helmet with full-face coverage. Besides the broken leg she was pretty bruised ups and scrapped but not as much as you would expect. She's lucky that side of the road was a mostly grassy field."

"How long ago did this happen?"

"Almost three months ago. Now that she can travel I want her closer to me and this is the place my wife found that we thought she would like. She's a little hard to please sometimes so..."

"I think I understand, and I'll talk to her about her leg and that part of it." Dr. Pete stood up. "I'm sure you would like to be on your way. Did I hear you're going on a trip and won't be here for a few weeks?"

"Yes, we're leaving for Italy at six-thirty tomorrow morning and we'll be gone until after New Years. I can email you my itinerary if you want it."

Dr. Pete smiled as he extended his hand. "Maybe that would be helpful in case something comes up, but for now just come with me and I'll have you check the contact info and we can revisit this whole staying situation when you return. And you do understand, since she's not mentally impaired, she'll be signing the residency and medical and financial papers. Didn't I see in that report that she is responsible for all of that?"

"You're so right. She doesn't want anyone else in charge of her. Not in any way."

Dr. Pete smiled as they left his office and walked across the hall. Sister Nora had the papers laid out on the counter and Willy pulled his pen from his pocket, ignoring the one laid out for him, and dutifully signed by the X.

"Thank you so much for your help Dr. Pete and Sister," he said as he put his pen back in his pocket. "And Good luck."

Sister Nora and Dr. Pete exchanged a glance and Dr. Pete said, "Good luck to you too."

Willy shook both their hands and left looking like the weight of the world had been lifted. Then he started to whistle. Bambi didn't like it when he whistled, but she wasn't here now, was she.

CHAPTER 4

Tuesday night's dinner at St. Francis was usually set on a theme and tonight it was Italian. There was Vegetarian Lasagna or Veal Parmesan; and a glass of red wine if you wanted, and Larry wanted. He could taste the almost bitter tang on his tongue and feel the warmth it would cause going down his throat, but happily Steve was beside him in line and nodded toward the wine. Larry nodded too, then shook his head no. Yes, he saw the wine, and no he wasn't having any. Not that it wouldn't be good with the Italian food but he'd been clean and sober now for just eight days short of two years and he wasn't going to backslide. At least not now.

"Does it make it hard on you?" Steve smiled at his buddy. "I mean seeing this wine and not having some?"

"Well it is a little hard sometimes, but not so much with wine. Now if they had martinis lined up I think I'd just give in. That's what I miss most, but my

AA counselor says it's what was associated with the martini I miss. The relaxation and the socialness it represents. Maybe he's right. The more I have a social life without it, the less I miss it. Does that make sense?"

"Does to me." They were at the end of the food line now and headed for their table.

The St. Francis dining room tables were placed with plenty of room to walk around them and as the guys made their way they said hello to several people. The big surprise was that there was a new person in the dining room. Almost everyone had heard she was coming and here she was, sitting at the table with Natalie Greene. The guys sized her up as they walked by. Her light brown hair was shot with very little grey, and cut short. She looked like an athlete, slim and muscular in her upper arms and she was sitting up very straight in her chair. They couldn't tell how tall she was but they could see the cast on her leg sticking out the side of the table along with the walker standing by. She wore no makeup but didn't seem to need it on her pretty face that belied her age, and when she looked up they could see her bright green eyes. Both men smiled at her but she didn't seem to notice. She looked back down at her plate and went on eating.

Larry thought she looked nice but Steve took special notice. A new woman, and certainly a woman of interest.

Steven Edgar Xavier was a connoisseur of women and at the age of eighty-four he had had his share of liaisons. Some were good and some not as good as planned, but he still loved women. Now a new woman was in residence and a new conquest was in his future. It noticeably perked up his spirit and Larry just smiled at him.

As they sat down Larry said, "Another one to add to your stable?"

Steve feigned surprise. "What do you mean? Oh, that little ol' sweetie sitting over there? Well, I'll certainly try to befriend her, her being a stranger here and all."

Both men laughed but Larry had no doubt that Steve would know her very soon. Whether they hooked up or not, Steve would enjoy the chase, as always.

And at *little ol' sweeties* table, Natalie was very busy trying to get information out of Pat. As her tablemate she felt it was her duty to know all the details. She knew her name was Patricia Olson and she knew she had a broken leg from an accident, and she knew that Pat's nephew was in Italy so that's why she was here at Haven Port, but that's all she was able to find out and this was unusual. Natalie Ann Greene, of the *don't forget the e on the end of Greene*, prided herself on her way with people. She could always make people respond to her, and this person, this Pat person, would not be an exception.

"We are so glad you picked St. Francis. Where did you live before?"

Pat barely looked up from her plate. "Portland."

Natalie already knew that. "Were you in a retirement facility there?"

"No. Do they have someone come around with coffee or do we get our own?"

"Well, we help ourselves. Do you need more? I'd be happy to get it for you."

Pat took the last drink from her cup and held it out to Natalie. "That would be very nice."

Natalie stood and picked up both cups. She could use more tea too. As she made her way across the room she decided that Pat could just take her own time filling in the story of her life. After all, they weren't going anywhere soon.

Sister Nora was making the rounds of the tables reminding everyone of the unscheduled and impromptu travelogue that Dr. Chu was offering in the meeting room at seven o'clock. He and his wife had just returned from a cruise down the California coast and they had lots of slides to share. When she reached the table where Pat sat alone she said, "Ordinarily Beth and Lyle Lee would be sitting here too but they're off visiting for a few days. They should be back tomorrow."

No response from Pat.

"Do you play Bridge or Pinochle? We have a group that meets on Friday evenings for cards and some play Scrabble and other board games."

"I did play Bridge but haven't for long time."

"Well, this is a good group to re-learn with." Sister started to leave the table then turned and smiled at Pat. "And when you finish dinner, would you mind stopping by the office to do the rest of the paper work and I'll give you a copy of the schedule of events."

"Sure."

Sister Nora walked away, mentally shaking her head. Pat sure wasn't big on conversation, and she wondered how Natalie would cope with that.

Natalie came back with a small tray holding her tea and Pat's coffee. She set it on the table between their places and than sat down herself. She was wearing a dark green wool pantsuit tonight and she was happily getting accustomed to the warmth and feel of wearing slacks in the evening. Her wardrobe was going through changes now that she was going out at night more often. She found slacks much more comfortable in this weather, and she still felt well dressed even when wearing a flatter heel.

"Thank you." Pat moved her cup back to the saucer.

"You're welcome. Did you know about the movie tonight? I'm not sure what's playing but it's usually something interesting. Last week we saw 'Pirates of the Caribbean.' A little raucous for my taste but all in all, it was fun."

"I thought there was a travelogue tonight."

Natalie pressed her napkin to her mouth. "Oh yes, they changed the program." And she had forgotten but it didn't matter. She had other plans. She was going out with James Pritchard III.

People were starting to leave the dining room and most would be going back to their own apartments to freshen up before this evening's presentation. Pat stood up and positioned herself in the walker. In her mind it was called *that damn walker* but it did what she needed for now, so she would tolerate its presence. On her way out of the dining room, she passed a happy couple holding hands and talking to a tall balding man with white tufts of hair sticking up on his head. All three looked at her and smiled. The woman said, "Hello. Are you getting settled?"

She answered, "Yes," and kept on with her slow walk towards the hallway.

"Well I guess we'll get to know her better in time," said Mary Engles. She was holding hands with Paul, her new husband of only a few months, and they were chatting with George Masters. Now that George had his new hearing aids and they were comfortable enough for him to wear all the time, he was learning to chat. In fact, he had become very friendly and was surprised at how many nice people lived here. Although he was a loner by nature, he'd known most of these people all his adult life and so it was more like reconnecting with old friends. Gone was Grouchy George and here was almost always friendly George.

"Going to the travelogue tonight, George?" Paul was looking up at the taller man.

"No, don't think I will. I've been down the coast plenty of times and there's a soccer game on tonight. I'd rather see that."

"We're going. We've been thinking about a cruise and this might be what we would like to do too." Paul and Mary moved a little closer together. This new marriage was so happy.

George noticed this move and felt a pang of loneliness. He seldom wished for a mate but now that he was more active in the community and could see the happy couples that lived here, *well, it might not be so bad to have someone too*, he thought.

"Have you ever been on a cruise ship, George?" Mary was looking up at him too.

George was taller than everyone that lived here. At six feet four he towered above most crowds and even the stoop in his shoulders didn't make him seem any less tall.

"Nope. Never did go. Wife was afraid of water. She almost never went on the ferry to Seattle for that reason. She just liked to be home."

"Maybe you'd like it. I'll get you information too when we get ours."

And George surprised himself by saying, "Okay." And he thought, *Can't hurt to look.*

As Pat came through the office door, Sister Nora picked up the folder with the typed name of Patricia Rose Olson on the tab.

"Here we go. How was dinner? Did you get enough to eat?"

Pat sat down in the offered chair and said, "Yes, plenty and it was good. You have a good chef."

Sister smiled. "We think so, and just so you know, Tuesday nights are always a theme night. Like tonight was Italian, next week is Thai food and the next week is Irish. If you have a favorite ethnic flavor you like, just let Edith know. She's always open to suggestions."

Pat was listening and couldn't help but be interested. This joint sure did try to make it less boring than that Portland place. "Do you need anything more than a signature?"

"I don't think so. Let's look." And they spent the next few minutes going over the insurance information and verifying Pat's ID, insurance contacts and all the numbers. At the bottom or the insurance page Pat signed by the X and then at the bottom of the Agreement of Occupancy she signed again noting that it was month-to-month contract.

"I realize this is not the normal 'occupancy arrangement' and I thank you for making it possible for me to be here."

"We can be a little pliable sometimes and this seemed like one of those. I hope you'll be happier here."

Pat looked at her. *What had she heard? Did she know about Portland?*

"If there's anything you need or you think I can help with, please don't hesitate to ask me or Dr. Pete or anyone on the staff."

"Thank you again."

"Well, one more thing. I noticed you didn't have a way to carry things on your walker so I found this carry-all. I think it's called an apron. It's got pockets so you could carry glasses or a book and Dr. Pete said he has an updated walker model for you. One with wheels so it doesn't take forever to move around." She reached over and slipped the apron over one of the curved handles. "Now, would you like to go to the travelogue? I can show you where the library is."

Pat smiled. She was delighted at the thought of faster movement and it had been a long time since someone had done something nice for her with no strings attached. "No, not tonight. I think I'll just go back to my room and watch a little TV. Thank you for being so nice."

Sister Nora smiled. "You are so welcome. I'll walk back to your place with you because I'm on my way to the library and I'll bring the walker to you when it arrives."

They left the room by going out the door across from Dr. Pete's office and back by the dining room door and down the hall to Pat's apartment. A very slow walk because of the walker that Pat was still getting used to using. Take a step, move the walker forward, take a step move the walker. When they got to her door, Sister said, "Okay, you're on your own until breakfast. They have coffee ready at six o'clock, and breakfast starts at seven and it's over around nine. If you want, you can take coffee back to your room but we hope you'll remember to bring the cup back to the dining room at the next meal. I've scheduled housekeeping for your room once a week on Mondays but if you need something like extra towels, let me or anyone in the office know."

Pat listened and thought, *Okay, now here come the rules.*

But that was the end of Sister Nora's speech she smiled and said, "See you later then," and turned and walked away.

Pat opened her door and walked into the apartment. She sat down on the couch and picked up the remote control for the TV and started surfing. *Guess I'll get the rules later,* she thought, then she found the station with the soccer game and turned so her legs were stretched out and settled in to watch Calgary get whomped by Vancouver.

CHAPTER 5

Everything at St. Francis was calm and serene this Tuesday evening but not in the neighborhood on Mercer Island where Willy lived. When he got home Bambi was very cool but not so cool that she didn't have something to say.

"Where have you been? Don't you know that there are things to be done before we leave?"

Willy was swaying just a little and his speech was a little slower than usual but he thought he was in full control. "I stopped at the Hilltop Club to have a drink. I needed to touch base with Albert and I saw his car so I pulled in. Now I'm cleared to take off. Aunty Pat is all settled and Albert and I are going to keep in touch by email so..."

And that set her off. "This is supposed to be a vacation from work. How dare you make arrangements to talk to Albert and did you say you'd call that Aunt of yours too? Make all those interruptions in our trip? You'll ruin everything." She managed to squeeze a tear out of her eye so it ran down her cheek, then she started to cry and it got louder as she ran to the bedroom.

Willy put his hands on his hips and stood where he was and listened as the tirade continued. *Here we go again,* he thought. He looked around the condo. The bags were all packed and lined up by the door and he knew that Ace Security was going to check their place daily. He knew the mail had been stopped and he knew Bambi's mother had all the pertinent info. What was the problem? He decided he'd have a drink and think it over and then realized he was hungry. They'd stopped at McDonald's at around ten this morning on the way to Haven Port but that was his last meal, if you could call it that. He crossed the living room and went into the kitchen, but he was still able to hear Bambi in the bedroom. She was doing that hiccupping thing she did when she ran out of tears but was still mad. He poured a glass half full of Black Label Jack Daniels and added a couple of ice cubes. Then he opened the refrigerator and saw it too had been cleaned and was empty except for a package with sliced Swiss cheese which he picked up. He opened the lower cupboard and took out the box of rye-crisp crackers and was munching on the crackers and cheese when Bambi finally made an appearance in the kitchen.

"Still upset?"

"Yes, but I guess I understand. You had things to tie up too. I was just worried when you didn't come home for dinner and..."

"Did you cook?"

"Well, no, but I thought we could order in some Chinese or pizza." She moved over to stand closer of him. "Is that all you want to eat?"

Willy put down his drink and reached for her. "It's not too late for a pizza," he said as he held her close and his hands started to wander. "Do you want to order or shall I."

She allowed him to hold her but she didn't respond. "I'll do it, and why don't you just go take a shower and put on your robe. That will give me a chance to launder all the clothes that are dirty and we'll come home to everything clean."

"Okay, and tell them to make it snappy with the delivery. I'm hungrier than I thought." As he talked he released her, picked up his glass and added another inch of Black Jack then headed for the bedroom. He was shaking his head at all this hoop-la but what the hell, his vacation was about to start.

And Bambi watched him thinking, *I'm back in charge.*

CHAPTER 6

Pat had a restless night but felt pretty good for having slept in a strange bed and the fact that she was trying to wean herself off the pain stuff. She got up at six and dressed in one of those one legged sweat pants she had too many of now, wishing again she could just pull on a pair of jeans and a sweatshirt and go running. She put on one sock and tennis shoe but wasn't sure how she was going to get the other sock on. Maybe she could impose on Sister Nora. She brushed her teeth, washed her face and hands, wet finger-combed her hair then headed out. If she didn't run into Sister before she got to the coffee pot, she'd look for her later.

When she got to the dining room she could smell the perking coffee at the back of the room just behind the serving wall and that's where she headed. Her therapist in Oregon always said step, pickup, place in front, step—repeat as necessary. Pat smiled as she remembered and as she rounded the corner she almost ran over Steve. His back was to her and it was a good thing her reflexes were up and running full steam this morning.

"Sorry," she said, then maneuvered around him to get a mug.

"Need some help pouring that?" Steve moved over and reached for the pot he had just put down. He poured the steaming coffee without waiting for an answer then said, "Sugar or cream?"

"Nope. Thanks for the help."

"No problem. Looks like we're the only ones up. Are you planning to stay here to drink it?" He was hoping for company. Not only would he like to get to know her, he really wanted conversation.

"I guess I just need to stand here and drink it. I can't seem to manage any move to anywhere else. They did put this little shelf here on this thing but who ever invented these walkers thought the user would be able to balance I guess."

"If you want to sit in the dining room I'll carry the cup for you and if you want to go back to your room I'll carry it there too. In fact, I'll bring my own coffee and we can get to know each other." If a voice can convey a leer, his did.

Pat groaned inwardly. He was hitting on her. Just what she needed. Some Lothario past his prime making a last ditch effort.

"If you would just take it to the first table inside, I'd be thankful and you don't have to keep me company. I'm fine."

"No problem. I was looking for someone to talk to and you showed up. An answer to my prayers." His smile was almost a leer too and she again groaned but not so much inside as before.

"Don't you want me to sit with you?"

"Look. I'm only going to be here a short time and your efforts at friendship or more are just wasted on me."

Steve just looked at her. She was some woman. Not angry at his advances, just very matter of fact. "Well. In that case, how about we start out just being friends. Can we do that?"

"If it will get me to a place to drink my coffee I'll say yes," and she started toward a tables in the dining room. Steve followed and set her coffee in front of her as she sat down at the first one she came to, then he sat down himself. "

"I know a guy that could fix a tray or something for that walker so you could carry stuff like coffee. Want me to talk to him?"

"Depends. What would I owe you then?"

Steve laughed. She was a good sparing partner for him. "Nothing in return. Maybe a conversation in the mornings when no one is up but us."

"Okay then I would like this guy to help me but what about him? What does he charge?"

Steve laughed. "You are so suspicious. It won't cost anything except maybe a kind word to him when he finishes the job."

"Okay, but be aware that if this is in any way a ruse to be more than a friend, then I'll bust you. Understood?"

"Understood. The guys name is George Masters and I'll tell him what you need as soon as I see him."

Pat picked up her coffee and took a sip. By this time, it was cool enough to really drink and she enjoyed it very much. Soon the cup was empty and Steve offered to get her another. She agreed and as they drank this second cup they actually started to chat.

"Yeah, I play Bridge on Fridays and I also like to play Poker at Murph's Place. Have you been here long enough to see it?"

"Nope. I've only seen the Catholic Church, the cemetery, a hotel, a corner of the golf course, and here. Oh yes... and I saw the ferry landing."

Steve laughed. "There are a few more things besides that. Like the Cliffs, the beaches, and of course Murph's. And there's Mickey's restaurant up north on Front Street and the mall. Hell, you have lots of places to check out. That is, as soon as you can really walk again."

"I don't think I'll be here that long but thanks for the rundown." She took a last drink and stood up. "I'll see you around." She positioned herself to leave then as she walked away Steve noticed she had a bare foot hanging out of the cast.

"Hey, don't you need to have something on that foot to keep it warm?"

"Yep." She kept walking. Take a step, pick up the walker move it in front of her, take a step, move the walker. Slow going. Crutches would definitely be faster.

"Do you need help putting on a sock or something?" He caught up to her.

"I'll find Sister."

"Sit down." He grabbed a chair and turned it around. "Sit down. I'll do it." He picked up the sock he saw hanging out of a pocket in the apron Sister had put on the walker.

She sat and he gently pulled the slipper sock over her swollen toes. "There. Feel better?"

He was being nice so she smiled. "Thank you." She stood up and started back down the hall.

He smiled too as he watched her slowly

maneuver the walker to her apartment then he headed for the smoking patio. When he opened the door and was greeted by a strong cold wind so he continued on to the smoking room. St. Francis did not allow smoking anywhere except in the smoking room and in nicer weather, on the patio that led to this room. He pushed open the door and found George reading the paper and enjoying his coffee with his morning pipe.

"Morning, George."

"Morning, Steve."

"Want some coffee? I brought a pot in with me."

"No, just had two cups in the dining room with that new gal, Pat."

"You move fast."

"I like to think I do but this was an accident. I was there and she came in with that walker thumping ahead of her. And that reminds me, she needs some kind of shelf or something so she can carry coffee or a tray on the walker. Can you figure something out? I know you're good with that kind of stuff and I thought maybe you could..."

"Sure. I can fix up something. Where is she now?" And George Masters *was* good at that kind of stuff. Being a Master Craftsman with granite and fine woods had been his life for many years and although he'd finally sold his company to his nephew, he still liked to work there off and on until his final retirement after his wife died. Besides the rock and stone and woods, he worked with metal too. Building and refurbishing those fancy offices in Seattle and at many other locales kept him busy for almost sixty years and now he would be happy to have even the smallest job to do. "Should I call her or what?"

"She's in the apartment by Sister's office. Why

not go knock on her door?"

George thought about that and then said, "Maybe I will." He finished his coffee and got up to leave. "Want the paper?"

"Any good news in it?"

"The usual stuff. Did you hear about the body that they found by the ferry dock?"

"Nope. Anyone we know?"

"Don't know. Not identified yet." He handed Steve the paper and left the room, but as he entered the main hall, George lost heart. He just didn't think it was proper to go knocking on that woman's door when they hadn't even been introduced. In fact, he didn't even know her name, so he went back to his apartment. Soon it would be breakfast time and he'd see to getting an intro.

Breakfast at St. Francis was busy this morning. Everyone seemed to be up early. By 7:30 the dining room was buzzing with talk, sprinkled here and there with laughter. George and Paul usually shared a table with two other guys but now that Paul was married and he'd moved to Mary's table, there was an empty chair at the four-person table.

George got in line and put a bowl of oatmeal, apple juice, and two slices of toast on his tray. As he walked to his table he saw the new woman come in. *How's she going to handle a tray?* he thought. Then the light bulb moment. He could help her and be introduced at the same time. He set his tray down on his table and headed toward her but before he made it across the room, Sister Nora appeared beside Pat and they got into the food line.

George sighed and just returned to his table.

As usual, after breakfast Sister made her

announcements: "Today is Wednesday and it's going to be a cool day. Temperatures in the low forties, and that wind is from the north so you know that means icy cold. Today at ten o'clock is crafts, and the trip to Seattle starts at ten-thirty when the van arrives. This month's outing is to the Seattle Yacht Club for lunch and the speaker is Commodore James Alexy from Lake Huron, Michigan. If you haven't signed up there is still space for three more people. And, tonight at seven we will have the movie that was previously scheduled for last night. The projector has been repaired and by the way, thank you Dr. Chu for stepping in to entertain us. Weren't those pictures that he presented beautiful?"

There was scattered clapping and many "yeses."

"Also, don't forget there will be popcorn available here in the dining room before the movie. And she finished with her usual smile and, "Have a Blessed and safe day."

This signaled the end of breakfast for many of the diners and clanking dish noises were heard as the residents took their trays back to the clean up area.

Pat stood up then sat down again. Same old problem. How to get her tray taken care of but when she stood up again she saw Sister coming toward her with a very tall man.

"Pat and George, I don't think you've met yet, have you?" Sister Nora smiled at both of them.

"No. I was just looking at her tray." George was blushing slightly. He knew that was a stupid thing to say but he didn't know what would be right.

"That's nice George. I'm sure Pat could use some help for a while. Pat Olson this is George Masters, and since you seem to have the matter in hand, I'll say good-bye until later."

She was smiling to herself as she walked away. *Another friendship shaping up*, she thought.

George just stood there not knowing what to do next.

"Hello. Thank you for helping me." Pat looked up at this tall, slightly stooped man and smiled.

He smiled back but said nothing.

"I can't seem to manage to carry anything with this contraption."

Again he said nothing but picked up her tray and started to the back of the room where the trays were put for clean-up.

Pat watched him walk away then started her trek back to her apartment. She was happy for the help and if he didn't want to talk, that was okay too. It took her some time to get out of the dining room and George caught up.

"Could you use a way to help carry things?" It was blurted out by a man who had little practice with small talk, especially to a woman.

Not stopping Pat said, "I sure could but I'll only be using this for a few weeks, then a crutch. I'll make out."

George walked slowly beside her. He remembered when his mother had had a broken leg and how long it took to heal, and then how his mother had needed to spend months exercising her leg and hip muscles to be able to walk properly. Of course his mother was a lot older than Pat. She'd been in her seventies but still. "I could put a little shelf on there so you could at least carry your tray and coffee. Would you want me to?"

"Are you a friend of Steve's?"

"Yeah." *What difference did that make?*

"He told me he had a friend that could do that

for me, so, okay."

George stopped and then took a long step to catch up again. "Could you stop so I could measure?"

Pat stopped and George pulled out his retractable tape measure and bent to his job, then stood up again. "I'll have this for you later today," and he turned and walked away.

She watched him go down the hall and out the patio door. *Okay*, she thought.

CHAPTER 7

The Haven Port Hardware Store and Lumber Yard was a two block walk from St. Francis, and for George and his long legs it was a quick trip. He knew the owner Brice White well and when he explained what he wanted to do, Brice led him to the scrap lumber pile and pulled out a nice piece of six-inch-thick teak. "Let's take it over to the saw room and we can fix you right up."

Following George's instructions, a hole was drilled down four inches from one corner with a notch for the cup handle, and grooves were made on the underside to fit on the tray, then the edges were smoothed out. "Want to stain this?" George said yes and Brice opened a can that was sitting on the paint table. "Will this do?"

"What is it?" George picked up the can and read the label. "Teak Guardian. I've used that before. Yeah, this'll do. It'll make the surface non-slip and it's waterproof. Yeah, this'll do."

George painted the board and then Brice put it into their drying kiln. "Got time for a cup of coffee while that cooks?"

George nodded yes, and as they headed for the coffee pot in the back Sheriff Ken Owens walked in the door from the lumberyard side of the building. "Hey, Brice. How you doin'?" The men shook hands and Brice said, "Do you know George Masters?"

"Sure do. His son-in-law's my neighbor. How you doin' George?"

"Gettin' along," said George.

"We're taking a break. Want some coffee?"

Ken said yes and Brice poured hot coffee for all of them.

"Heard about the body by the ferry. What's the deal?" Brice sat on a high stool and indicated the other stools for them.

"I don't have much time to talk but we found the body of a woman. No ID yet but we're working on it." He handed Brice an invoice and said, "I need some two-by-fours and a couple of other things delivered to the Sheriff's office today. Can you do that?"

"Sure. I'll have the kid run them over after school. Is that soon enough?"

"Yep." He took another drink then sat his coffee cup down still more than half full and said, "Well, the stuff I need is on the list and if I'm not there, someone will be. Just need them off-loaded into the garage. Okay?" He handed Brice the work order and started back out the door.

"Okay." Brice wondered if this could possibly have anything to do with the woman they found but already knew that he'd heard all the info that Ken was willing to tell. At least right now.

The Sheriff left and since George was a man of

few words Brice knew there was no need for conversation as they finished their coffee. When the timer rang they both set their cups down and headed for the kiln.

Brice pulled the piece of wood out and they looked at it with critical eyes. "How's this?"

"Nice," said George. "What do I owe you?"

"Nothing. This was a scrap of wood and the finish was the end of someone else's can, so this is a freebie. Besides you gave us all that equipment when you moved so I guess we still owe you."

George was flushing a little. This was nice. He should come over here more often. He missed working on things like this. He'd look into doing something here after the holidays, but being a man of few words he just shook Brice's hand, said, "Thanks," then walked out the door with the new shelf under his arm.

A few minutes later he was standing outside Pat's door. He'd been there a couple of minutes, trying to decide if he should knock or just wait until lunchtime, when Dr. Pete saw him.

"Hello George."

"Hello." Then he remembered the piece of wood under his arm. "I made this for Miss Pat so she could carry things. Would you give it to her?"

"Why, isn't she home? Have you knocked?"

George looked down at his shoes and got that rosy cast to his cheeks again. "I didn't knock. I didn't know what to say when she answered."

Dr. Pete stepped forward and knocked. From inside they heard, "Just a minute." And, in just about a full minute, Pat opened the door.

"George has something for you," said Dr. Pete, and so do I. I'll be right back."

Not saying a word, George thrust the board at

Pat. She immediately knew it was for the walker and said, "Come in and see if it fits."

George started in and realized Dr. Pete wasn't following. He turned with a sort of pleading in his eyes but Dr. Pete was already walking away.

"I won't bite you George. Come in."

He walked straight to the walker, settled the board between the hand pieces and took a step back. "It won't be slippery when it's wet and it won't warp."

Pat made her way slowly toward the walker by hanging onto the furniture. "This is beautiful. How did you do it so fast?"

"I know the guy at the lumber yard and he let me use some equipment. It was easy to do."

"You should go into business making these for us gimps." She laughed and to her surprise, so did George.

"Something to think about isn't it." He looked down at his feet and said, "Well, I better go."

"Want some juice? I was just getting ready to pour. It's apple."

George smiled. It was his favorite and he had planned on getting some before he went back to his place. "Thank you. Yes, I would." Too late he realized this would require conversation but decided maybe he could just let her talk.

While she poured she was thinking what a nice thing George did. Not many people in her life did nice things for her. Then contrary to what Steve had said, she started to wonder what was in it for him. What would he want from her?

"I'll help you bring it over," George said and picked up both glasses as she hobbled over to the recliner. She got settled and he handed her the glass and sat down himself. No one spoke.

They drank and then drank again and still no one spoke. Then at the same time they said, "Did you see..." and they laughed.

Pat said, "This is a little awkward, isn't it? We don't know enough about each other to even ask polite questions so I'll go first. I live in San Diego and had an accident while riding on my motorcycle and here I am. Now you."

"I've lived here on Haven Port most of my life." Then he thought maybe he should say more. "... and moved to St. Francis after my wife died."

"Okay, my turn. I have been married but that was so many years ago I've forgotten what it's like to have a partner."

George looked down at his shoes. Something he did often. He hadn't forgotten. His wife was one of those perpetual happy people. Perky and full of life and how she got married to this grumpy Norwegian was beyond everyone's understanding. But most of his grumpy-ness came from the fact that he never could hear well, so instead of embarrassing himself, he just didn't talk. It wasn't until he was in his sixties that his wife finally put her foot down. He thought it was a waste of money. People should just speak up, but she really insisted he get hearing aids, and so he had the tests and started the process. However, it wasn't long after that they discovered her cervical cancer and then leukemia and then she was gone. He never went back to get those first hearing aids fit properly and so they were uncomfortable, and of course he didn't ever try to get used to them. They always lived in his pocket and until this summer he'd really never heard what people were saying and in turn he was half-mad all the time because people talked so low. Then his daughter finally put her foot down too. "Dad, you're missing out on your grand-kids. You're so grumpy they don't want to come see you, and I think it's because you can't hear." So, with Dr. Pete's help, George got the proper care and instructions and now that he could hear he was constantly amazed at how much he enjoyed television and even sometimes, talking to people.

Finally, he answered Pat. "Having a partner is good if it's the right person."

"I agree but being single doesn't mean we can't have friends. Now your turn, what did you do before you retired?"

"I owned a company that built the insides of offices and those fancy homes. You know, slate and granite and woods, like in beams and floors and banisters and stairs."

"Wow. No wonder you could build this shelf so fast. Did you build stuff in any buildings I might know?"

"Well, the Portland Conference Center, and in Vancouver there was a bank, and in San Francisco there is a theatre and lots in Seattle and other places."

Pat took another look at this George. She had totally misjudged this balding, tall man who walked with a slight stoop that made you think his back hurt. He was an artist in disguise.

Abruptly George stood up and put his glass on the table.

"Thank you again for the shelf. It will be so helpful." Pat smiled at him.

He got a little rosy but smiled too. "You're welcome." And he moved to the door and left.

Not much for small talk, she thought, *but very interesting.*

When Dr. Pete left George, he went back to the office and looked at the walker standing in the corner. He would take it to Pat shortly but first needed to make a call. As he reached for the phone, it rang. "This is Dr. Pete." He listened then said, "Oh, hello." Then another pause. "Sounds good. I'll ask her and let you know, but I'm sure we can make it. Thanks for asking." He listened again then said, "Okay, see you Sunday. 'Bye."

He disconnected, got a dial tone and hit number one on his speed dial.

"Hello?"

"Hi. It's me. Want to go to a Sunday cocktail and dinner party and concert at the Estate?"

"I think that sounds delightful. What time?"

"It starts at four." Dr. Pete was smiling, thinking of his Emily standing by the phone. He always thought of her as *my Emily*, and very soon they would be married.

"Are you still coming for dinner tonight?"

"Yes. I'll be over about five. Want me to pick up anything?

"Nope, the roast is ready for the oven. See you soon. 'Bye."

"Good-bye." Dr. Pete was still smiling when Sister Nora came into his office.

"It's nice to see a happy doctor. Anything special?"

"I just talked to Emily and that always makes me happy. What can I do for you?"

Dr. Pete sat down. He wasn't an especially tall man at five-feet ten inches, donn he wasn't especially good looking, but he had that caring look that showed in his face and demeanor, and when he was happy, as he had been these last few months, it made his hazel eyes sparkle, and that made him handsome.

"I'm so glad about that. What I wanted to discuss with you is what exercises Pat is supposed to do. She was asking Steve about going to the gym. Can she do that?"

"I'll talk to her. It might not be a bad thing if she minds some basic rules about the leg. I have something to give her too. Do you know where she is now?"

"In the dining room, I think. They were in the food line for lunch when I overheard the conversation."

Dr. Pete got up from his desk and together they walked down the hall. Sister Nora was an inch taller than Dr. Pete, with wide athletic shoulders that told of her Scandinavian heritage just like the pale yellow of her hair. Had she not had her own caring demeanor, some would have thought her a formidable woman.

CHAPTER 8

Sheriff Owens drove out of the lumberyard that Wednesday morning about 9:00am, and headed back to the ferry landing. The investigation was never really over in these kinds of deaths. Not until the bad guy was found. He smiled to himself. *Because of all those detective TV shows, everyone thought every mystery had an ending* he thought, and hoped that there would be an ending for this one too, and soon.

Kenneth Owens moved back to Haven Port several years ago, after he retired from the FBI. Then, after he'd joined the sheriff's office, he'd finally felt he'd found his niche in life. The first twenty-six years of his working career was for the government and he thought he was ready for retirement, but after only a year he was not only bored, but he was actually getting tired of playing golf every day, so when Sheriff Robert Nelson asked him to fill a deputy vacancy, he was ready. Then two years later when Robert had the heart attack, Ken was the one that filled in as Sheriff. It was just a matter of an election to get the paper work in place and now he'd been at it for almost thirteen years. Haven Port is where he'd grown up and gone to high school. He knew everyone who lived on the island full time, and most of the summer people. It was his town and he was sure as hell not going to sit around when a dead woman showed up.

He walked around the old driftwood stump that stood next to the path and then went down the bank between the present day ferry landing and the old one that had been out of commission for over thirty years. He stood there a minute thinking. He wasn't seeing the peninsula across the water, or the mountains in the background, or how the sun sparkled on the waves, nor was he seeing the three people fishing off the old dock, or even the ferry boat that was just leaving. He was seeing again the scene of yesterday and the body of the woman floating by the piling.

Haven Port Island is located in the part of Puget Sound, in-between the Kitsap Peninsula on the west and Seattle on the east. The ferry dock was on the south-west side of the island and, except for private boats or small planes, this was the only way to get to Haven Port. As the sheriff stood there he thought, *11:00am ferry from Seattle brought in the body. At least that's the way it looked. And when the ferry left Haven Port, part of her clothing was snagged by a piece of cable sticking out of the piling and she unhooked from the ferry and stayed here.* In the few minutes he'd looked at her he'd noted she was around forty-five to fifty years old, had bleached blond hair and was not a thin woman but not very large either. Her clothes looked expensive and the one earring she was wearing looked like diamonds and some other blue stone. Her nails were long but several looked like they'd been torn off. Like fake nails. There was one shoe, no handbag --- that would have made it too easy to make an ID --- and he'd seen a small heart shaped tattoo on her right ankle. And, he just realized, she wasn't wearing stocking either.

He took a notebook out of his jacket pocket and added to his notes:

Tattoo new? Identify
Check Missing Persons report
Check fingerprints report
Check clothes for tags

He put the notebook and pencil back in his pocket and headed up the bank towards his car. His next stop would be the Medical Center. The autopsy should be finished by now and maybe the doc could give him more info to work with.

Several lookey-loos were standing across the street and he smiled at them as he got in the car. He marveled again at how fast word spread on the island, and the Seattle newspaper got wind of the story too, so there'd been an article in this morning's edition. The people on the island were great walkers so he had no doubt that most of them would make their route down by the scene of this latest excitement.

Ken parked his car by the Doctors Building, picked up the folder marked FERRY LADY from the passenger seat and got out. He smiled at the title on the folder. Ethan's work, he decided.

The Doctors Building and the Haven Port Hospital behind it took up two whole blocks and a sky bridge connected them. The ground floor of the front building held the Mental Health and Public Health department along with an emergency room. On the second floor were the labs that served not only the hospital but also the sheriff's department on those rare occasions when they needed those services, such as an autopsy.

Dr. Pete was just coming out of the building. "Hey Ken. Out doing Sheriff's work?"

"Yeah. Busy morning."

"I was just talking to Curly about your lady at the ferry dock. He's finished with the autopsy and has a couple of interesting things to tell you."

"Can't wait to hear. See you later Pete," and the Sheriff walked in the side door

He took the elevator up one floor and stopped at the reception desk. "Dr. Curran, please."

"Hi, Sheriff," said a sweet young lady whose name tag read CK. She picked up the phone and punched a button. "The Sheriff's here to see you." She listened a second, then said, "Okay." She hung up the phone and smiled at the Sheriff. "Go on in. He's in his office."

Ken smiled at her and wondered at the way these young working women seemed to get younger every day. He knew this one was married and lived in one of the cottages on the east side, just below The Cliffs, but with her hair in a ponytail she looked to be about fifteen. When he got to Dr. John Curran's office he said, "'Morning Curley. How old is that little dark haired receptionist?"

The doctor looked up. "Hi, Ken. In her twenties I think, why?"

Since high school, Dr. John Curran had been known as Curly to all his friends because he wore his hair long and it had a frizzy, curly, and a totally unkempt fright wig look. Now he wore it short but it still was that blond frizzy cap of curls.

"They just look younger every day," the sheriff said, and they both laughed. "What can you tell me about our ferry lady?" He sat down in the chair beside the desk.

"Five foot five, approximately one hundred sixty pounds, and she wasn't in the water long enough to get bloated. She didn't die of drowning, and she had a piece of skin caught in her mouth by her back teeth, like she'd really bitten someone very hard."

"That's different. Anything else?"

"Isn't that enough?"

"It's a good start."

Curly chuckled. "Okay then I'll tell you the rest." He ran his fingers through his hair as he talked. "She had track marks on her arm too so she was a user and that's something to consider. I haven't finished the blood workup yet but I'll let you know what she used or was on."

"Can the skin piece be analyzed? Is it big enough for DNA?"

Curly sat back in his chair and said, "Sure. Smaller things like hair follicles can be used for DNA. I've already sent it to Seattle to the FBI lab. It'll take a few days but maybe we'll get lucky. Oh yes, another thing, inside the tattoo on her ankle were the initials DAM. Could mean something or just be a statement on life, I guess." Both men smiled.

"How about those fingernails?"

Curly picked up a piece of paper and said, "They were those fake things that beauty shops put on and they're glued pretty tight. Looks like she was in a fight when they got torn off, and oh yeah, she had a bruise on her right jaw bone that looks like someone hit her."

"Did Tom come by?" If was standard procedure to have a representative from the Sheriff's department stand in during any suspicious-cause-of-death autopsy.

"Yeah, the deputy was here and I gave him all her clothes. Here's the list. One coat, one dress, one shoe, one earring, one pinky ring, one earring with a stone, one bracelet, and that's it."

"Wait. Did you forget to list the under clothes?"

"Nope. There weren't any. Not even a bra. Surprised Tom and me too."

Ken put the list in the folder with the other papers. "That all you have for me?

Curly looked at his desk and said, "Yes. I gave you the clothing list and oh yeah, here's the list of things I sent off to get tested."

"Thanks." The Sheriff stood up and so did Curley.

"You going to the cocktail party at Pritchard's on Sunday? My wife's so excited. She likes to hear that Simpson kid play the piano." Curly was running his hand through his hair again.

"My wife says we're going too. I like his music but..."

"Hey, if the wife wants to go, then what choice do we mere husbands have?" Curley put out his hand and they shook.

"Right. See you at The Estate on Sunday," said Ken and he headed back to the reception area and elevator. He was thinking about Sunday and the party and hoping this case would be finished by then.

CHAPTER 9

The Pritchard Estate was a prominent site on the northwest corner of the island in an area locally referred to as The Cliffs. John Pritchard was as close as the island came to having royalty. His family had owned this Estate since 1901, when Captain John Pritchard the First, built the house for his bride and eventually filled it with his eight children. John Pritchard II was also a sea-faring man and his wife Eleanor came to love living here too. They moved in after their wedding because both of John's parents were ill. His Mother had severe arthritis and many other illnesses that defied identification, so Mary became their caretaker and mistress of the house and raised her own three children at the Estate.

John Pritchard III was not only one of those children but was the last male in this line. He'd never married but his nephew Edgar Bruce Simpson lived with him. E. B. Simpson, as he is known in the world of famous musicians and to his fans, was a pianist but when his touring career was cut short because of a fiery automobile crash, he'd became a permanent resident at the Estate on the Cliffs. Periodically a musical cocktail party or afternoon tea party or a dinner party was held and E.B. would play, but since his accident left his face so terribly disfigured he only recorded his music and never again toured. When he felt the need for a live audience he swathed his face in a white bandage type of mask. In private he joked he looked like the Invisible Man but he never wanted the public to see his scarred, distorted face.

E. B. read about the woman's body being found and thought maybe a little excitement was finally happening here on the island, so when he took his morning walk it was down to the scene, bandages in place and hooded sweatshirt pulled up around his face. Several others were standing there by the dock already, chatting and wondering out loud about who or what. A man with light brown was also there. He had almost blond hair and was wearing sun glasses but didn't really stop to look, nor did he speak to anyone as he continued walking slowing through the small crowd that had gathered, however he too was wondering how in hell her body found its way to this island.

The crowd had dissipated somewhat but those few left watched as the Sheriff came, parked, looked and then drove away, and since there didn't seem to be any excitement left, the man that lived on Front Street and grew beautiful roses started home, the two couples visiting from Canada walked back towards their motel discussing in French what they had heard about this incident, and as Murph drove by he too wondered about the whole deal.

Michael Murphy was the owner of Murph's

Place, a friendly little bar and restaurant not far from the St. Francis Retirement Center, and almost across from the golf course. Murph and Sheriff Ken had gone to school together here on the island and even to the University of Washington, and when Ken went to work for the U. S. Government, Murph became a policeman in Seattle. Their paths hadn't really crossed again until Ken moved back to Haven Port and then Murph moved back too, only four years ago after he was hurt during a drug bust. He still carried a bullet in his back but on most days it didn't bother him much. He pulled into his restaurant's parking lot and when he got out he noticed a flyer posted on the tree. *Will cut grass, pull weeds, run errand, anything. 555-1807. Todd Fisher.* Murph looked around and realized this could be a good thing. The blackberry bushes were growing too close to the sidewalk and beside the building, and the grass around the parking lot sure could use cutting and trimming on a regular schedule, not just whenever he felt like it. He knew Todd's dad and unlocked the door thinking what else he could have the kid do. Windows needed washing and the back steps needed replacing. He wondered just how talented this kid might be. He stopped at the phone in the bar and called the number. "May I talk to Todd please?"

"I'm Todd," said a very deep male voice. Murph thought maybe he'd gotten the father so he said, "Hi. This is Murph. I'm looking for Todd junior."

"That's me. Hi, Mr. Murphy."

"Hi." Murph hesitated. He thought Todd junior was a kid. "I saw your flyer. I need some stuff done around here at Murph's Place. Got time to come by and talk to me?"

"Sure thing. When's a good time? I could

come now."

The kid was anxious to work it seemed and Murph liked the sounds of that. "Yeah. Now would be good. Come on over."

He hung up the phone and started turning on lights and the coffee pot he'd set up last night. The bar side of Murph's Place opened every morning at nine, but the restaurant had been open for a couple of hours. He could smell the Irish potatoes cooking and especially the onions, and that made him hungry. He lived above the restaurant in a nice little four room apartment but last night he'd stayed at Lisa's house and that cup of coffee he'd had there was just begging to be joined by breakfast.

He walked into the restaurant side and said, "Hi Betty. I'll have the usual." Two eggs over easy, bacon and Irish potatoes, and as he picked up the paper to take back to the bar, in came Todd. Murph thought, *I never would have recognized him.*

"Hi, Mr. Murphy. I'm Todd in case you don't remember me."

"I remember you but not, well not this big. Didn't I see you last summer?"

"No sir. I've been living with my mother in Seattle for a couple of years, but I'm here now. Moved back right after Thanksgiving."

"Are you still in high school?"

"No sir. I'm at the U. That's why I'm back here. I got an internship in the Ichthyology Department here on the island and it starts in January. I just thought I'd earn a little spending money while I can."

Murph laughed. "Good idea. Have you had breakfast? Want to join me and we'll talk about what I need doing."

"Yes sir. I had breakfast with my dad at 5:30

but I would have a cup of coffee."

Murph smiled again. "Okay, but first thing you need to do is call me Murph and stop calling me sir. It makes me feel older than I already feel."

Murph laughed and Todd smiled.

"How old are you? I was going to sit in the bar, are you old enough yet?"

"Yes sir... I mean Murph. I turned twenty-one last week. I don't drink but just sitting in a bar is okay, I guess."

Murph led the way and they sat at one of the tables. He took a closer look at this young man. He probably stood six feet, had light brown hair and dark brown eyes, which were just a little almond shaped. Murph remembered that Todd's mother was Vietnamese and his father was a big Swede from Minnesota. It made a nice combination. "Let's talk about what you can do."

It turned out Todd had worked last summer for a carpenter so definitely he could fix the steps, he would wash the windows inside and out, and cut back the blackberry bushes and mow. Then there was some painting that was needed and new shelves to be installed and, well, after that they would see.

Todd was happy. He was hoping to find some place to keep him busy and make some money and Murph was happy to find Todd. They settled on Murph paying a fee per job, and by this time Murph was finished eating. He showed Todd where the yard clippers and mower were kept and after they settled on this jobs price, Todd started to work. Murph figured this would be an all day job so he told Todd that at noon he was to come in for lunch, and along with the pay he'd get one meal a day for the days he worked here. Todd liked that too.

Murph was behind the bar ready to pour another cup of coffee when Larry and George and Steve walked in. "Hi fellows. Coffee with or without?"

"I'll have without," said George, Steve and Larry just smiled. Everyone knew he was a member of AA and it was coffee without forever more.

"Hear about the lady in the water?" Larry stirred sugar into his coffee. "Wonder who she is?"

"Yeah I heard but I don't know anything more. I was hoping Ken would drop by and fill me in but I guess he's busy today."

George was sitting on the stool just listening. Since he got his new hearing aids he knew what was being said but just listening still worked pretty well for him, and no one seemed to mind.

Larry took a sip of his coffee then said, "I heard it wasn't anyone from the island so I guess no one has been reported missing."

Steve said, "Sure is interesting, isn't it?"

Murph nodded. "I heard that too and yep. A mystery right here in front of us."

They chatted for a few more minutes about what they had heard then Larry said in his best lawyer voice, "Well, maybe this is all the excitement there will be. Body found, body goes back to Seattle, forget body. Case closed."

"If it's no one we know I guess that's okay." Murph reached for the coffee pot again and poured for all three. "What else is new?"

"Got a new gal at St. Francis," said Larry.

George perked up at the mention of Pat.

"Oh. Someone we know moved in?

"No. She's from California." George joined the conversation. "Had a motorcycle accident and needs to mend."

Murph and Larry looked at each other. They had never heard George speak about anyone like he was talking about her, and he was smiling.

"Got your eye on her, do you?" asked Murph.

George started to get a rosy glow. "No," he said and picked up his coffee cup.

"Hey, it's okay to find her interesting. I just hope you can corral her before Steve moves in." Both Murph and Larry laughed but not George. He knew Steve had a way with the ladies and that Pat was nice looking and that Steve liked nice looking woman and.... *Oh crap*, he thought. *I guess if Steve wants her, I'll be out of the picture.* Now he was frowning.

"Hey, cheer up ol' buddy. You have the inside track so far with the shelf you made her walker. All's not lost yet." Larry and Steve were laughing but George didn't seem amused.

Murph picked up the remote and turned on the TV. "Let's see if there's anything about the excitement on the news." He switched channels and found the local news. "...and it looks like identification hasn't been made yet. In other parts of the Sound today, three fishermen had a little too much fun and drink early this morning and had to be rescued from the rocks off of..." Murph turned down the volume. "I think we just missed what we wanted to hear but doesn't sound like they know anything new," and Murph switched to the weather channel.

The three men turned their conversation to the nice weather pattern being talked about and then Murph told them about Todd going to be around helping out.

"Do you know his Dad?" Larry asked. "He's a nice guy. Lives in that little house just around the bend from the golf course and commutes to Seattle.

He's really fixed it up nice. Looks like a country cottage with the picket fence and swing on the front porch. What ever happened to his wife?"

"She moved to Seattle and took the boy with her about ten years ago. Don't know any details but things happen. The kids nice too. Even calls me sir." Murph laughed. "I told him I'm not old enough to be a sir." All three men were laughing as Todd walked in, hat in hand.

"Mr. Murphy. Can I talk to you a minute?"

The three men laughed again.

"Who's Mr. Murphy. I'm Murph, remember?"

Todd reddened slightly. "Sorry. Can I talk to you a minute?"

Murph walked to the end of the bar and Todd said, "The sheriff came by and asked me if I could do some diving for him again today. I told him I was working for you but he said to ask if you could spare me."

"Of course. The bushes can wait. If you can come back today, just let me know."

Todd smiled at the other men and stuck out his hand to Murph. As they shook he said, "Thank you. I'll be back or I'll call you." And as he went out he put his Mariner baseball hat back on.

"Must be something about the body," said Larry and the others nodded. "Wonder what they're looking for?"

CHAPTER 10

Todd saw the sheriff's car parked at the side of the road in front of the old ferry dock. He pulled his Jeep Patriot up behind it and started to unload his diving gear.

"Hello Todd. Thanks for coming. The ferry is just about to come in and I'd like you to check the sides, well really all around it, to see if you can tell if the body was hooked on it or just how it brought the body over. I don't have much hope but we need to check anyway now that we know which ferry it was."

Todd nodded and started putting on his wet suit and today he would wear a helmet with an air supply, light, and a built in camera and microphone that fed into a recorder in his vehicle. He was ready in a few minutes and he walked down toward the waters edge to put on his fins.

Vessels in the Washington State Ferry system are all named for local areas and some after the local Indian Tribes. There is the Spokane, the Issaquah, the

Snoqualmie, and this one was called Suquamish. It came into the dock as usual, sort of coasting in then the engines were reversed to bring it to a smooth stop, just nudging up to the dock. Deck hands were securing the off ramp and three cars were ready to off-load onto Haven Port Island.

The Sheriff made the necessary arrangements beforehand so the ferry captain of this boat would wait for his specific directions before taking off again. Todd entered the water and turned on the camera to start his search. He waded in backwards then turned and swam to the far corner of the ferry. As he worked he talked into the recorder. "Front left corner: Escape ladder in place and secure. No lashings free, nothing to catch and drag." He slowly moved down the side of the boat and rubbed his hands over the surface as he went. "No obvious or visible signs of disturbance on left side." He turned the corner and continued his search along the back of the boat. He pulled and shook anything that was sticking out and said, "Back left corner: All gear seems to be secured." Then he dove a little lower to go under the decking. "Back right corner intact."

Sheriff Owens stood by the open door of Todd's car watching the monitor and listening to the dialogue.

"No visible marks on this right side but wait a minute. There's a line loose and hanging down by this front corner. Make that the right front corner and the line is thin cable. The escape slide and chute seems okay and secure but there's a piece of rope sort of looped and hanging out right next to the cable that's hanging. Maybe this is what hooked the body. I'm moving to the front to get a better picture and then I'll move to the top and bottom." There was silence for about five minutes then, "Okay. I'm coming in now

Sheriff, if that's okay."

Todd saw the universal okay sign the sheriff made with his thumb and first finger joined and came out of the water. He removed his fins and as he approached his car the sheriff was releasing the tape.

"Thanks Todd. Just what I needed. I'm taking this tape with me to get a copy made. I'll let you know if I need any further diving. Thanks again." He'd already released the disc from the machine, slipped it into an envelope and was starting towards his car, when he remembered he needed to go into the office and saw the boat captain was there waiting for him. "Hi, Stan."

"What did you find? I saw the diver paying extra attention to the front corner," said Stan Peterson, captain of this ferry.

"There was a line loose. Looked like something came undone from the escape slide. How often do you check those things?"

Stan took off his hat and rubbed his balding head. "Supposed to be checked once a month unless there's something to warrant an extra check. Like these last storms we had or a bump or something."

"Well it's hanging down now and might have been yesterday too. Who checks it?"

"Supposed to be a OS. We got some new guys, maybe they missed it. Can I continue on to Seattle now?"

"Does OS mean deck hand?"

"Sort of. It stands for Ordinary Seaman.

I have no authority to hold you but will you call me when you find out about the maintenance and inspection? That body didn't come by itself and since we found it after this ferry left yesterday, I'm betting you brought it over."

"Well, not me specifically but I know what you mean. I'll get back to you ASAP," and he put on his hat with the Washington State Ferry logo on it and headed back to his boat thinking, *I hope it wasn't that stupid kid from Texas that screwed up again.*

That kid from Texas wasn't due back to work until shift change the next evening at seven, but you could bet Stan would get to the bottom of this and just minutes after he docked in Seattle, he was on the phone to the Washington State Ferry Office of Personnel.

"Stan Peterson here. Is Fred in?"

Fred was on another line and so Stan left a message for a return call, but he wasn't waiting patiently. He was fuming. *Those stupid people that hire deck hands have to have their heads up their ass. Here's a case of sending a kid from Texas to work on a boat without making sure he knew what to do. Who was running those training classes anyhow?*

Before the boat was finished loading and new batch of cars on board, the call was returned.

First the hellos then, "Fred, we got a situation here." And he explained about the body and what had been discovered. "That dumb kid I've been complaining about was on that crew yesterday. I'd bet he didn't check the safety slide or the cabling after the drill like he was supposed to, and after that storm it probably got lose. If that's the case, I want something done about him."

"Calm down, Stan. Let me look into it and I'll get back to you. What boat you on?"

'You know damn well I'm on the Suquamish, and I wasn't captain yesterday but not..."

"Don't worry. I'll get back to you."

They both hung up. Stan still feeling angry and somehow responsible, and Fred was thinking, *if that kid is at fault, he's outta here. Union or no union.*

And at the Shipyard Hotel where the kid from Texas was living, the nightly poker game had already going-on in the lobby. It had started in the late afternoon but T.J. joined in as soon as he got home from dinner and a few drinks at his favorite tavern just down the street. It was nearly 12:30am when he was playing his first hand. After the betting was finished he said, "I got three Jacks. I win." And he reached for the pile of bills.

"Not so fast sucker. Look what I got here." This man sitting across from him displayed his massive forearms by rolling up his tight fitting, black tee-shirt sleeves to his shoulders. He wasn't a big man but decidedly a man that worked a physical job that kept his body rock hard and bulging with muscles. He spoke with a thick Russian accent and he glared at T. J. as he laid down his Ace-Queen-10-9-7, all spades. "I got Flush. That mean you get nothing." He made a dirty, phlegm filled sound that probably was his laugh, and raked in the pile of money.

T. J. was afraid of the Russian, but he'd had just enough to drink that he had what his Father called Dutch Courage. "I think you cheated. I saw you pull cards from the bottom of the pile before and I think you did it again." T.J. stood up and so did the Russian, who wasn't overly tall but looked formidable with his bulging arms and neck muscles, and his face was dark with rage.

"You call me cheater?" he yelled. The Russian made one swing with a closed fist and connected with the side of T.J.'s head. Those twenty-five years of building muscles sent the smaller man across the room, sprawling on the floor. T.J. didn't move and didn't get up. He was out cold. After a signal from the Russian, two of the players picked him up and took him back to his room. "That will teach little boys not to call me cheater," said the Russian and he made that sound again that he thought was laughing.

And T.J. didn't wake up for a long time. Not for almost seventeen hours, and when he did wake up it was to pounding on his door.

"Hey. You got a phone call."

"Okay." T.J. rolled off the bed and stood up and then sat down again. His head was ringing and when he looked at the door, it was a fuzzy. "Be right there." He stood up again and headed for the door. He was feeling his way by putting his hands on the wall and as he walked toward the phone at the end of the hall he thought, *I need more sleep and some aspirin.* "Hello"

"Is this T. J. Jackson?"

"Yeah. Who's this?"

"This is the Washington State Ferry personnel office. Were you aware you missed your shift today?"

T.J. looked at his watch. His shift didn't start until seven this evening. "What do you mean? It's only a little after eight. You woke me up."

"Sorry I woke you, but it's almost eight-fifteen in the evening. Your shift started at seven. Do you plan to come in to work?"

T.J. wished he could sit down. Now his stomach was feeling rocky and he thought he was going to throw up. "Are you sure?"

"Yes I am. Are you sick?"

"Yeah. I think I am."

"Okay I'll put you down as sick but you better come into the office tomorrow before you check in to get all squared away. Do you understand?"

"Yeah. I'll come in tomorrow."

He didn't realize he'd hung up before he answered, and as he felt his way along the wall back to his room he wondered again what was wrong with him. Then he remembered the poker game and how it ended. He also remembered why he'd been afraid of the Russian. After seeing him beat up some lady on that fishing boat as the ferry came into the pier, he'd vowed to keep away from him. He wasn't sure the Russian had seen him watching but even if he had, this was too much. That stupid Russian wouldn't get away with this. He'd figure out a way to get this taken care of, but right now he needed to go back to bed.

The Russian watched as T.J. talked on the phone then as he made his way back to his room and realized this was the face he'd seen watching him when he was taking care of business. *But,* he thought, no *problem there. That little boy would be more respectful next time we meet* and he was sure too *this rabbit was too scared to open his mouth about anything he's seen.*

CHAPTER 11

Steve was looking for Pat. He finally found her in the upstairs solarium reading the Seattle newspaper. "Hi. What you doin'?"

Pat looked up from the paper and smiled. "I'm making a pie to take on a picnic. What do you think I'm doing?"

"That was a stupid thing to say, wasn't it? Want to get some coffee? I was looking for some company?" Steve sat down on the chair next to her.

"I think I had enough coffee at breakfast but I'll go have juice while you drink coffee." She liked Steve. He was up front about wanting and needing conversation and she understood that. Sometimes you just needed a human being and the sound of their voice. She herself was pretty self-contained but more and more she appreciated having just a someone to talk to for no reason. Not talking to get information, and not having to watch what you said, and not having to worry about who was listening was satisfying to her now for some reason. She stood up. "I travel pretty slow these days."

"I have time to walk with you. Anything in the paper of interest?"

"Been reading about that woman that the ferry brought onto the island. Do you know anything about it?" Pat was still trying to get used to this slow pace. Even with the new walker that had wheels, it was slow going. She was getting faster but still it was tedious and a little painful. She longed for the day when she could just stand up and walk somewhere.

"I don't know much more than the paper says. I know they had the diving team checking the ferry yesterday and that they found something. Don't know exactly what, but a guy I know said the Sheriff took the tape recording the diver made, so he must have reported something."

"Do they know who it is yet?" She'd looked at the sketch in the paper and thought she might know her, but wondered if anyone else did yet, and she also wondered just how it could be Charlene. Last time she'd heard about her, she was on her way to jail in North Carolina and that was around five years ago.

"No ID yet." They were off the elevator and almost to the dining room door. "Say, how about a cup of tea instead, and some of those cookies they just put out? Anita just made oatmeal with raisins. They're fresh out of the oven."

Pat agreed and as she picked out a table and as she sat down she pondered the news article. She decided she'd check on the ID of this woman when she went back to her room. The laptop was all set up now and she'd just do a little research.

Steve came back with a tray just as Mary and Paul came in.

"I could smell those cookies clear upstairs," Paul said. He turned to Mary, "Want tea or coffee?"

"I think I'll join Pat with a cup of tea."

She turned to Pat and said, "Hello. We sort of met yesterday. I'm Mary Engles and that is my husband Paul. Do you mind if we join you?"

Steve spoke up. "Course not. The more the merrier." And he pulled out a chair for Mary. "Mary and Paul are newlyweds. They got hitched last summer. He chased her until she caught him." Steve thought this was funny and laughed but both Pat and Mary just smiled. This joke was just too old.

"Congratulations. Did you just move here too?" Pat decided she better get to know the people that surrounded her and the only way to do that was to ask question.

Mary laughed. "No, we've both lived her for a few years but we just decided to get married. We knew each other's spouses too so it's not much of a change from good friend to husband."

Paul was returning with a tray and heard the remark. "Well it might not be much of a change for you, but for me it's a great deal better than being alone."

"That's not what I meant and you know it," Mary said and smiled at Paul. A little teasing was very pleasant and their marriage was very pleasant too.

"Hey, did you see the drawing of that woman in the paper? Did you recognize her?" Steve said.

"I don't' think she's from the island. Neither of us ever saw her before. How about you? You'd be the one to ask about any woman on the island?"

Steve smiled. "You're right about that but I don't think I ever met her either."

"Then for sure she's not from here." Paul

laughed and Mary and Pat smiled. He bit into a cookie. "Now this is just what I thought it would taste like."

"What makes you so wound up today?" asked Steve. Paul was usually a little on the quiet side and a fairly reserved.

"Well we made some big plans this morning. First we got asked to a party on Sunday then we made reservations for a cruise in February. Guess I'm just jumping around inside with joy about being able to travel again, and with Mary."

"Oh yeah, that's why I was looking for you this morning Pat. Want to go to a cocktail party and musical soiree on Sunday? John Pritchard and his nephew invited me and told me to bring a guest. Would you be my guest?"

Steve's look was hopeful and a little pathetic for such a Romeo, Pat thought.

"Oh, do come," said Mary. "It's really fun when JP gives a party up at the Estate, and the nephew is E. B. Simpson, the pianist. He lives here now after his car accident. Still records but doesn't tour any more. Once in awhile his uncle, James Pritchard, we all call him J. P., invites people in, and E.B. plays. And the food is wonderful too."

"I thought you said cocktail party." Pat was looking at Steve.

"Yes, I did say that. They serve booze at both or do you mean about the food? Well, it's more like a cocktail party with a dinner too. Sorry I misled you."

Pat had been to many embassy teas and other so called cocktail parties that were more like suppers so she understood, and she thought it just might be interesting to meet this hick town's nobility. "Sure I'd like to go but I don't have anything to wear. With this leg I can only manage sweat pants. Of course I could wear my diamond tiara. That would sparkle things up."

"If you don't mind wearing used clothing, I think I have something that would do. You're shorter than I am but we could adjust that."

Mary to the rescue thought Paul. *No wonder I love her so much.*

Pat smiled. What a nice woman to help someone she hardly knew. "I'll take that help." Then she turned to Steve and said, "Yes, I accept your invitation. Tell me what time to be ready."

Four happy people sat chatting about past parties and making plans. Steve would drive and as Sister Nora walked by the door she was happy too. Pat did seem to be fitting in and making friends. Maybe those reports of how difficult a patient she had been were overstated. She didn't seem to be a problem here. Or even un-nice.

CHAPTER 12

Thursday

Charlene's picture was being noticed by someone else too. The Russian ran his hands through his hair and absently scratched his arm pit. It might be time for him to disappear again, and most certainly if the paper discovered who she was and where she'd been.

He picked up the paper again and read the article. *Haven Port Island. Huh.* He'd never been there but it was just across the bay and maybe worth a trip. The shipyard whistle blew to signal that the lunch break was over. He threw the paper in the waste can and picked up his hat. *Da. Tonight I take a ferry ride.* He chuckled his phlegmy sound. *Maybe I see the little boy who see's me on fishing dock.*

Murph's Place was not only a bar and restaurant but a very favorite gathering spot for the locals. Because

Haven Port was an island, almost everyone knew everyone else, if only to nod to, but at Murph's it was pretty much always the same crowd that had know each other for years and exceptions were few, however, one exception was Brad. He'd been part of this local scene only six months or so, but he worked at the University Satellite campus and had been introduced to Murph's by a couple of regulars so he quickly become one-of-the-crowd.

Todd, the kid Murph hired to do work around the place, was busy cutting back the blackberry bushes at the edge of the parking lot when Brad pulled in and parked. Todd knew who Brad was but had never been introduced so he just kept hacking away with the machete.

"There's an easier way to do that, you know. If you hold the handle with both hands and move your body like this, you get two whacks for the price of one exertion."

Todd turned and looked at Brad. That made sense and he hadn't thought of doing it that way but, why not give it a try. He grasps the handle with both hands, and made a couple of swings, seeing that this two sided machete worked very well that way. "Thank you, sir. That is faster and maybe easier too."

"I spent my share of time in the jungle chopping through vines and that's about as bad as these black berry bushes I think." Brad smiled and patted Todd on the back. "But I'm glad I don't have to do it anymore. I'll leave it to you young guys," and he turned and went in the door.

Murph was behind the bar. "Hi Brad. What'll you have today?"

"I think I need a beer after watching that young man working so hard on the bushes. Who is he?

Haven't seen him before."

"Names Todd Fisher. Just moved back to the island. Been living in Seattle but going to start an internship here at the U so he's back living with his Dad. Nice kid."

"Yeah. Been a long time since anyone called me sir."

"His father's retired military so he grew up learning how to address us elders, but it makes me feel older than I want to admit to."

"I know what you mean," replied Brad but then they were distracted as the sheriff came in.

"Hey Ken. Coffee?"

"Please."

As Murph set the cup on the bar in front of the sheriff he said, "Have you met Brad?"

"Can't say that I have." He took stock of this man he'd been aware of but never formally met. This Brad guy appeared to be in his late forties or early fifties, nicely dressed wearing a dark tan suede jacket, jeans and cowboy boots. Ken offered his hand and they shook. "New to Haven Port?"

"No, been here awhile but I travel a lot so it's sort of hard to meet everyone."

"Brad works at the U. Studies earthquakes." Murph filled the coffee cup then drew another beer for Brad. "Just got home again, didn't you?"

"Yesterday. And I came home to find Murph working on his landscape." Brad didn't like to talk about himself so he changed the subject. "Prettying the place up, huh?"

"Yeah, I saw Todd was back to work. Sorry I pulled him away yesterday but we needed to do a little checking." The sheriff took a drink of coffee. It tasted good. Murph's coffee always did taste better than even his own coffee at the office and even at home.

"No problem. He's here on a job to job basis. Sure a hard worker. I'm glad to have him. Did he help you find something about the woman?"

Brad didn't noticeably move, but he was very interested in the answer.

"Maybe, but can't tell yet. Can't really discuss anything either." He took another sip of coffee and decided to ask, "What do you do different to your coffee. It always tastes so good."

Murph laughed. No secret. I just put in a piece of lemon peel with the grounds. Seems to make it smoother or something. Got that from a bartender I had here once. Remember Scotty?"

"That was a while ago."

"Yea, almost five years. After he died his widow told me the secret. He never would."

Brad was just listening and wishing they would get back to talking about the body. He wanted to know where the case was headed. Would Seattle authorities take over or would local law enforcement here take care of it? And how much did they know?

The sheriff took one last drink from the cup and put a dollar on the bar. "Well, gotta go. Thanks for the coffee. See you later." And he left.

They watched as he passed in front of the window, got into his squad car and drove away.

"Excitement on the island, huh?" Brad took another drink of his beer.

"About as exciting as it gets here, I guess. They found a body by the ferry dock yesterday. She's not from the island so that's as far as it goes. All any of us know is what we read in the Seattle papers and you heard the sheriff, no news there either. So I guess we got ourselves a genuine mystery."

Brad laughed. It was expected so he laughed. He was good at reading the situation and doing what was the norm. "Well, I guess I'll get myself a paper and get caught up. Any left here?"

"Here take this one. I've read it. Not much to know but there it is." Murph pushed the untidy paper toward him.

"Thanks." Brad took a five dollar bill from his pocket and laid it on the bar. "Well, gotta go too," and he picked up the paper and left.

It was seven-fifteen and the Russian was standing on the deck of the ferry as it was pulling into Haven Port. He was taking in the surrounding terrain, and listening as the deck hand was pointing out to a female passenger just where the body was found floating. "Don't know who it was yet but she didn't live on this island."

"Maybe she was visiting?" said the woman.

"Maybe," said the deck hand then excused himself to ready the platform that would extend to the dock and allow passengers to walk off.

The Russian didn't get off. He could see nothing to concern him here, at least not at this time, so he went back into the cabin and ordered a beer at the bar. It was a nice evening and he would just enjoy the ride as the ferry continued on to the peninsula and then went back to Seattle. He strolled over to a window and sat down in a vacant chair at a table occupied by two ladies. It wasn't long before these women got up and left. He would never know that along with his body odor he also made them afraid. His dark hair was uncombed, he had a two-day growth of beard, and he had a fearsome scowl on his face. However, had he known, he would have enjoyed that fact too.

CHAPTER 13

On this Friday night at St. Francis, there would be some couples playing Bridge and some playing Pinochle and some playing Scrabble in the meeting room. Pat was going to join the Bridge players at the urging of Mary. "It's fun and not too serious. Sister said you used to play and everyone here is so nice, if you make a mistake it's not the end of the world. We all think of this as just cards, not life or death."

But, this was still Friday afternoon and Pat was standing on one foot, holding onto the counter and Mary was measuring the hem on a pair of bell-bottom dressy pants that would fit easily over the leg cast. "That's good. I'd hate to be killed because I bid wrong." She smiled and saw that Mary was smiling too.

"I think that's why we only have cookies and not pie for afterwards. No weapons like forks or knives." Mary stood up. There. I think that will be okay and I'll just whip them up on my sewing machine. Need help taking them off?"

"No, I can manage but I'll have to sit down." She hobbled and hopped into the bedroom and before she sat on the bed she lowered the pants with their elastic waist down to her hips. Then she sat and Mary pulled them off, taking care not to dislodge any of the pins she had just put in the hem.

"Thank you Mary. I wish you would let me pay you for those and for the shortening."

Mary stopped and turned around. "These are a gift and the shortening will only take about ten minutes. You can repay me sometime if I need a favor. Now, I'm going to leave you, do you need help getting dressed again?"

'No, I can handle it. And I owe you," said Pat and was still smiling at the wonder of having such a nice thing happen to her. More and more she was enjoying St. Francis and the people here, *even against my will*, she thought. Recuperating here was turning into not only an interesting time, but a happy time. It had been a long time since she'd felt happy, and another thing, she was excited about Sunday when she would wear the newly shortened pants. It had also been a long time since she'd had a date and she wouldn't have admitted it to anyone but she liked Steve and was looking forward to seeing him out of this retirement home atmosphere.

George had heard about the date too and he was upset. He feared that Steve would move in on Pat as soon as he could, but for some reason George was hoping Pat liked him more. *Oh, well. Guess I just don't measure up.* He was alone in the smoking room and when Steve came in he got up and left.

"Something I said," joked Steve.

George didn't say anything, just went back to his room, got his coat and hat and headed out for a walk. It was times like this he wished he had a project to work on. Something to do with his hands and that would keep him from thinking. He went out the front door with no destination in his mind but walked north, toward the corner then turned and headed across the street to the lumber yard. *Maybe something going on there*, he thought. As he walked into the workshop connected to the lumber storage building, he saw Deputy Ethan Mitchell holding court.

"Yep. Those kids found the body but they called us right away. A good thing too. The ferry brought her in, and the ferry could have taken her out again." He was sitting on a stool talking to the small group of men in front of him. "The boys were properly debriefed and sternly told not to tell any one what they saw. Sheriff Owens said I could interrogate them further if needed."

"But didn't they just see the body after the ferry left?" A very round, bald man seemed interested in this story.

"That's classified info but I can tell you that it was a woman."

"We already know that. It was in the paper. Have they identified her yet?"

But before he could answer Sheriff Owens came out of the office and said, 'Ready to go?"

With obvious reluctance the deputy nodded his head and followed the sheriff out the side door.

"Wonder how much he was supposed to tell us," said the bald man and then he laughed along with the others.

Brice saw George and said, "Poor Ken has to

fight the battle with that one. He doesn't seem to know what confidential means unless he doesn't know something."

George smiled. He had the same impression.

"How you doin' today George. Can I help you with anything?

George looked at Brice and said, "I need something to do with my hands. I'm getting a little bored this winter. Got anything for me here?

"Boy, are you ever an answer to my prayers. Yes, I do have something for you specifically. I got an order from a home out on the Point that wants some newel posts for their stairs. I was just trying to plan a way I could get them done and not have to work nights. Let me show you. They're talking about rosettes too but let's look at this first." He led George over to the office and George spent the next two happy hours with Brice. The first hour was looking at plans and discussing the project and the second making out orders for wood and setting a timeline for finishing. They also talked about the rosettes and decided they should go to the home in question and take a look then decide rosettes or not. George left the lumber yard a different man. He once again had a project that made him happy and he'd be doing something useful. When he got back to St. Francis he headed for the dining room for a glass of juice and ran into Pat, there for the same purpose.

She took one look at his happy face and said, "You look like you just struck gold."

"Well I have in a manner of speaking. Want help with the juice?"

"No, thanks. A friend made me this nifty holder for my walker and I can manage. Got time to sit and chat for a minute?"

Steve as already sitting at a table but took one look at them and decided he wanted his coffee out on the smoking porch and left. *These two might need to do some connecting,* he thought.

George smiled. "Sure," he said, but what he meant was *You Bet. I have things to tell you*

They took their apple juice to a table and George took off his hat and coat.

"Where you been?" asked Pat.

"Been to the lumber yard. I got myself a job." And he told her the story of walking in

and being offered this perfect project.

"Good for you. I can't wait to see the finished pieces. Or will I see them? Do you think you could bring one here or could I go there?"

George was smiling. "I'll work it out."

They sat chatting about the type of wood he would use and when he could get started and Larry came in. He got a cup of coffee and then came back into the dining room. "Mind if I sit down?"

Both Pat and George were surprised to hear him speak. They hadn't even realized he was there.

"Sure, sit down," Pat said. This was something new. Pat thought she always knew what and who were around her at any given time.

"What's so interesting that you didn't see me?"

George got a little pink but said, "Well, I'm going to do a project at the lumber yard and I was just describing it to Pat. Making some newel posts."

Larry smiled. He knew George was a master of wood working, and he also knew how shy George was, not only around women but that he generally didn't talk much to anyone. "Good. They're lucky to get your skills for this job. Who're they for?"

"Some house out on The Point. They're doing some refurbishing and this is for their stairway." He smiled thinking again of all the happy hours ahead of him.

"What is The Point?" Pat looked from one man to another.

"Out west of town. It a narrow piece of this island that someone decided to buy up and then build expensive houses around a nine-hole golf course. They have a gate and everything. Real classy joints." Larry took a sip of coffee. "Do you have to go out there George?"

"Probably when I get 'em finished. I sure I hope I get to install them too."

It made Pat and Larry smile too. Here was a happy man.

"Playing cards tonight?" Larry asked.

George and Pat both looked at him.

Pat recovered first. "New topic, huh?"

That made George smile, then both Larry and Pat joined him.

Larry continued. "I am. Do you play Bridge or Pinochle or any of that stuff?" Larry looked at Pat and she smiled then she looked directly at George.

"George do you play Bridge?"

George got rosy again and said, "Used to. Haven't for years."

"Me neither. Let's go learn again tonight."

George not only smiled but his eyes got soft and a little shinny. "Okay. Let's do that."

Pat stood up. "I'll see you both at dinner."

But she didn't get far. Dr. Pete and Sister Nora met her in the hall and happily exchanged her old mode of travel with the new wheeled variety. This new walker was the same manufacturer as the old one so the new table-top George made fit perfectly and Sister re-settled the apron for carrying things on the sides too.

Pat just stood by wondering at her luck. People who cared, people who worked to make her feel better and best of all, people that didn't seem to want anything in return.

She started her unhurried trip back to her apartment but still smiling and enjoying the easy way she could just walk and push, no more picking up. It was then she realized she was doing a lot more smiling and laughing then she'd done in a very long time too. And as she neared her door she also realized she hadn't finished her research on the picture she'd seen, and she felt she really did need to know where Charlene had been and how she ended up here. And how she got dead.

CHAPTER 14

The Friday Night Games were in action. One card table held the Scrabble players, and at another table the Canasta Players were making their melds and laughing at something that was said. At the two tables of Pinochle players on the far side of the room they were laughing and being as loud as the Bridge tables had come to expect, but no one tried to shush them anymore because it did no good.

Some people came to play Bridge with a partner but as Pat walked in Mary met her at the door.

"I think George is going to play tonight too. We were going to be partners," said Pat.

"Wonderful. Come sit at our table. We'll just save a place for him." Mary pulled out the chair and then moved Pat's walker to the side of the room. "I'll go get it if you want to use it between games."

"Thank you." Pat smiled at this very kind woman. "I think I can manage to get from one table to the next if I have to. How do you manage the partners changing thing? Sister Nora told me that you changed partners every so often."

At that moment George came in. He looked freshly scrubbed and for once his hair was combed instead of standing in tufts on his head. Mary motioned him over.

George said, "Hello. I'm not sure this is a good idea. I haven't played since, well since I was alone."

Paul patted him on the arm and said, "Don't worry. It's like riding a bicycle. You never forget and we'll help you until it all comes back."

George looked at Pat. "You still game?"

"Well, I'm here and it's too much trouble to leave so...." She was smiling up at George as she spoke, thinking she liked having him for a friend.

George's smile was wide and as he sat down Paul said, "Mary was just going to explain the changing partners thing we do. That way you're not stuck with the same partner all night and you get to know other people."

"We use a method for changing partners called Couples Switch. With four players per table, you start the first round with your partner but keep individual score cards. A round means playing four hands with this partner, then you total up the scores, write down your score on the appropriate line," and she showed them on the score card where round one, then round two, etc. should go. "And change partners at your table. After playing with the other three people, the two players with the highest scores move to the next table and play another set with new partners. This way everyone plays with someone different for each set. By the end of the evening, the individual with the highest score is the winner. And to add interest, each player puts a dollar into a bowl, and at the end of the evening the first place score receives ten dollars, the second place five dollars and the poor person who ended up with the lowest score receives the last dollar as compensation. If there is any money left we donate it to St. Francis."

Both Pat and George seemed to understand.

"I'm a little fuzzy about bidding..." started George.

"Oh, I almost forgot," said Mary. "I went to the office and made you a copy of this Cheat Sheet. It tells you what you need to bid and what to answer to tell your partner what you have." She gave one to Pat and slid the other across to George. They both picked up the half sheet of paper and started to read.

Natalie Greene was in charge of tonight games, as usual, and she stood up and said in her best *I'm in charge voice*, "Everyone at the Bridge tables ready? We all seem to be here. Let's begin. Start the deal."

Pat snickered then looked at George. "Sounds like the beginning of an Indy car race, doesn't it?"

George chuckled. He hadn't made the connection but he thought it was funny too and the others laughed because of George.

Paul picked up the deck and fanned the cards out face down in the middle of the table. Each player picked a card and George won the deal because he drew the Jack of Diamonds, and that was the highest card.

Paul reminded him that the person on the right needed to cut the cards and with that done George dealt the cards and the game began.

With gentle reminders of, it's-your-turn-to-bid and don't-you-have-any-trump-left-in-your-hand, the group had a good round. The bidding seemed to come back to George all at once and Pat was right with him.

At the end of this first round, Pat and Mary had the highest scores and moved to the next table.

Paul patted George's arm again. "So glad you got those hearing aids fixed. Look how much better life is for you."

"Someone should have kicked me in ass a long time ago, I guess." George was a little rosy around the cheeks but he was smiling. The next two players came to their table and Paul fanned the cards out again to see who would deal.

As Pat and Mary sat down after their move to the next table, Mary made introductions. "Dr. Chu this is Pat Olson and you've met Natalie, haven't you?"

"Why of course she has. She sits at my table and we have had many pleasant conversations," Natalie said.

Dr. Chu smiled at Pat as they drew for the deal. "I understand you are just re-learning the game so don't be afraid to ask questions as we go."

Natalie immediately sat up straighter and said, "Are you a beginner?"

"Oh yes. Very beginner. I played quite a bit in my younger years but not so much now."

"Don't let her lead you astray. She is remembering just fine," Mary said. "She was the one who moved remember and she got a pretty good score."

Pat looked at Mary. Such a sweet soul. Pat hadn't run into many of these in the last twenty years.

They played the next round and this time Dr. Chu and Pat moved to the next table. Steve was at this table and Pat got an introduction to Dolly McBride. Pat was definitely not surprised when this small woman with the wispy hair and the petite frame spoke with a southern accent. She wondered where she was from but before she could ask the cards were being dealt and they were playing again. This round also went smoothly and although Pat wasn't the high score, it wasn't bad.

Another hour of playing and it was time for the prizes to be awarded. "Patricia, you did well for just coming back to the game," Natalie said. Then she tapped her pencil on the table and announced the winners. "Dr. Chu is first, here's your money CC. Steve is second," and as she handed him his five dollars she said, "and although there is no money for it, Patricia took third place."

Everyone clapped. Some said 'good job' and others just smiled but they were all happy for her, and especially George. He was beaming so that you'd thought it was him that had won.

"And the *too bad* prize goes to Margaret Chu."

Mrs. Chu smiled and accepted the dollar and made a big show of putting it into here purse. "I'll spend this on my next trip," she said and it brought chuckles from almost everyone.

George retrieved Pat's walker and said, "Ready to get some coffee or tea?"

Pat smiled at him. "No I don't think I'll stay. I'm a little tired." She patted George on the arm. "See you tomorrow," and she started her slow walk to the door and down the hall as George stood watching her go.

Pat went into her apartment and immediately sat down at the computer. This afternoon she'd intended to start her research but got sidetracked by sitting down in her recliner first. She'd taken a pain pill and unfortunately gave in to a nap instead of her intended task. This laptop was certainly not the newest version available, but it worked okay for what she wanted to do. She signed onto the internet and then typed in the passwords that would get her to the government site she needed. In a few seconds that seemed a lot longer, Pat typed in a user name and then another password. Next, in the space provided, she typed in the name Charlene Black. Up came a message *No Match.* She typed in Charlene Brown. Again, *No Match.* She tried Charlene White, *No Match* then Charlene Grey and bingo, a match. Pat knew Charlene had many aliases and always used a color for her last name. Grey seemed to be her latest choice.

The screen showed Charlene Grey, and a booking picture that showed her with uncombed dark brown hair, a swollen and black left eye and a swollen lower lip, but she was still recognizable. The text under the picture stated she was five feet five inches, weighed one hundred fifty-two pounds and her age was forty-three. Pat looked at the date. Just as she remembered, Charlene was sent to prison six years ago on a ten-year term. *Must have been let out early.*

Pat clicked on a couple of keys to delete her path on the net then pushed *log out* and sat back as the computer closed down. That's what she'd been worried about. Charlene was out and had probably gone back to working again for that Russian faction. She needed to call her old partner. She'd know if this in any way would comprise her position and identity or if flight was in her near future. Having worked all those years for the Department of Homeland Security and then working undercover for the FBI after she retired, well, there were a few people she'd rather not advertise her whereabouts to and if Charlene was here, the Russian might be too.

She made a mental note to get a safe phone tomorrow. Maybe find one in the mall.

CHAPTER 15

When Pat work up this Saturday morning, she saw that Haven Port Island was hosting another windy, rainy storm from Alaska. The temperature was just about thirty-eight degrees with the wind chill said to make it feel around twenty.

"Not a fit day for man nor..." Dr. Pete was talking to Sister Nora when Pat came around the corner.

"Morning. How are you this beautiful day," asked Dr. Pete.

"I think your use of the adjective beautiful might be miss-used," said Pat.

Dr. Pete laughed. "Maybe you're right."

"Dr. Pete, could I speak to you for a minute?"

Sister Nora took the hint and said she had something to take care of and left.

"Sure. Want to come into my office?"

Pat said yes and started toward the door. Once they were seated Dr. Pete offered her coffee which she declined but she said, "I need a cell phone. Can you help me?"

Pete smiled. Of course he could help and he wondered why she didn't just use the phones here. "They sell the phones and service over at the shopping mall. Would you like me to take you over there?"

Pat thought, *good. If Dr. Pete bought it, it couldn't be traced back to her.* "Could you just pick one up for me? It's so much trouble getting anywhere. I'll pay you for it..."

Dr. Pete interrupted her. "Well, you need to sign papers and things. If you want, we could go this morning. The mall opens at ten."

Pat thought about it and decided it probably wouldn't matter if she did buy a phone. Not many people knew her real name anyway, just the company she worked for. "Yes, thank you. Should I meet you here by the door at ten?"

Dr. Pete nodded and Pat stood up and slowly walked to the door. "And do you have any idea when I can trade in this thing for a crutch or cane?"

He chuckled. "Looks like you have that walker just about mastered, but maybe next week we could check into an overhaul of the cast and a crutch. I'll make the arrangement for an x-ray to see how things stand."

"Thank you again." Pat turned and started down the hall. Now she would have coffee.

And on this rainy Saturday morning and T.J., the kid from Texas was back working an early shift on the ferry. T. J.'d gotten a warning put in his records for missing a day and not calling in, and he'd have to do extra training that he wouldn't get paid for. His head still hurt pretty much all the time. A dull, middle of the head kind that sometimes made his vision blurry, but he couldn't take any more time off because he didn't have any sick leave left. It had been so convenient to go out and party then call in sick that he'd used it up fast. Next month would bring more sick leave but that wouldn't help now.

As the ferry boat prepared to leave the Seattle dock, T.J. looked up at the Passenger Waiting Room windows. To his surprise, there stood the Russian, watching him. *What the...* he thought. He moved to the side making sure the docking ropes were secure and started to quickly walk to the other end of the ferry but when he looked back, the Russian was gone. He never had been a very deep thinker and with his head hurting like it did, he soon forgot that he should be worried. In fact, he forgot about the Russian altogether as he threaded his way amongst the cars and went to his post on the opposite end of the ferry.

Pat and Dr. Pete drove into the underground parking area of the mall and he found a space right next to the elevator which they took up to the first floor.

"Do you need my help?" Dr. Pete said as they entered the mall?

"No, not really. Would you rather wait in the car?"

"No, but while you get your phone, I want to pick something up at the jewelry store. I'll be right back."

Pat said, "No problem," and started her slow walk down the corridor. Dr. Pete crossed over to the other side.

As he entered the store he heard, "Hey Pete." The man behind the counter was smiling at him.

"Hello. How's things today? Got my watch ready?"

"Sure do," and he went to a table at the back of the store and returned with a box. "The hands just needed a little tweaking. Something must have gotten in there to make it stick. Maybe you should take it off when you have patients."

Dr. Pete nodded. "Okay. What do you think got into the watch?"

"Don't know for sure, but it seemed like some sort of hard dust, like mica or something like that. Been out doing some mining?

Pete smiled. "Not exactly. But could dust from a cast do that?"

"Well that's sort of chalky but maybe from one of those new plastic ones with that fiber they add. Had anything to do with those kind of casts?"

"Yes, and that's probably it. Thanks. What do I owe you?"

The jeweler smiled and said, "Nothing if you can get me an introduction to one of your friends. I've been trying to meet Natalie Greene but I can't seem to be at any functions where she is and if I am, she's with someone. Really I've met her, but I'd like to ask her out and I think..."

"I think I understand. Let me work on that and I'll get back to you in a couple of days."
Pete was smiling when he left the jewelry store. *Wait tell I tell Emily about this.*

Pat was finished with her business too and the young man at the cell phone kiosk was showing her how to check to see about missed calls. "...and you just press SEND and it shows what calls were made last. Who called you and also who you dialed, with the number and all. Any more questions?"

Pat said no and put the phone in her pocket and handed the box back. "I don't need this. She looked at

Dr. Pete but was still talking to the young man. "I have the cord for rejuvenation and the ear bud but I'm not driving so I don't need the one for the car and I'm sure you can get rid of the box and all the trappings that this came in."

"Sure can, and thanks for coming in. Let me know if you need anything else."

Dr. Pete noticed she had put the cords in her jacket pocket too. "All ready to go? Any more shopping you'd like to do?"

"No, I'm good to go. Can't wear anything except these sweats and they already feed me too much at St. Francis so, let's head out," and she started toward the elevator to go back to the parking lot.

"First time I've taken a woman shopping and we only got what we came for. Your something for the books." Dr. Pete pushed the down button and looked at Pat. She really was something for the books all right, in many ways.

CHAPTER 16

It was a little after eleven when Mary knocked at Pat's door and waited. No response so she turned around to leave when she saw her coming down the hall.

"Hello Mary. Looking for me?"

"Yes. I have your outfit ready for tomorrow." Then she noticed that Pat was all bundled up in a coat. "Been outside?"

"Dr. Pete and I went to the mall. I needed a phone."

"Isn't he the nicest man. Do you feel like trying these pants on again? If not, we can wait."

"No let's get it done." Pat unlocked her apartment door and went in followed by Mary who was carrying the two pieced pant suit on a hanger.

Pat took off her coat and then went into the bedroom to take off her sweatpants. Mary helped her put on the newly shortened pants of the suit and then slip on the shoes that Mary had given her earlier.

As Pat stood up the silky material of the pants

slid down her leg and when she looked in the mirror, she was pleased. Part of her old self was evident and Pat even smiled at the reflection.

Mary was happy too. "Want to try on the jacket now too?"

"No, I'll wait to see the whole package later. I'm ready to get this leg up. Can you stay a few minutes?"

"Of course. Lunch isn't for half an hour." Pat struggled back into her sweat pants and they returned to the living room. As she settled into the recliner where her leg could get supported, Mary hung the suit in the closet than sat on the couch. "I'm excited about the tea party tomorrow. We'll leave here about four forty-five and..."

"Wait a minute. Aren't we supposed to be there at five?"

"Yes, but it's not very far away. Nothing on the island is very far away." Mary chuckled. "From one end to the other is about a twenty-five minute drive and across is shorter.

"I thought this island was bigger. Listening to people talk about the Cliffs and then out at the Point where George is doing that job. I guess I need to take a tour."

"It's not going to be much of a tour but it is beautiful and really it's the people that make it feel bigger. We're so diversified in what we like and what we do. When you're ready I'd be happy to take you around and talk my head off."

Pat smiled. Again this woman that didn't know her was going to put herself out to help, or at least spend time with her and show her around. Another nice thing.

There was a knock at the door and Mary said, "Shall I get that?"

Pat nodded and when the door was opened, there stood George.

"Hello George. Come in, I was just leaving," said Mary.

George looked at Mary then at Pat then back at Mary. "Okay," he said and stepped into the room.

"I'll see both of you at lunch," said Mary and she went out the door, closing it behind her.

"Sit down George."

"I was just on my way to lunch and wondered if you would like to take a ride this afternoon. With me, I mean. I have to go out to The Point to do some measuring. Just so you could get to see more of the island." He was blushing and didn't seem to know what to do with his hands. First they were in his pocket then at his side then clasp in front of him then back to his pockets.

"What time did you plan to go? I went out this morning and I'm a little tired but if I don't have to do much walking, I'd like to go."

George's word came out in a rush. "No walking, just riding until we get to The Point then you can sit in the car of else come in and see the house. Not much walking." Now he was holding his breath waiting for her reply.

"If it's around two o'clock, I'd like to go. I need to elevate this leg after lunch so would that work out?"

"Yes it would," said George then he turned, opened the door and was gone.

Pat smiled to herself. George was really one of the old guard of gentlemen and so shy. But she liked him and now she needed to get ready for lunch. She hefted herself out of the chair and made her way to the bathroom then the bedroom where she'd left her walker. Once again she wished for jeans and running shoes instead of what she was wearing. Especially the running shoes.

At lunch George watched as Steve stopped by Pat's table and chatted. He tried not to be jealous, but he was. He was still worried that she would fall for Steve and not want to, well, to do whatever he could get her to do with him. He watched as they smiled at each other. Were they making a date? Then he watched as Sister stopped to chat then Mary then Dr. Pete. *Okay,* he said to himself. *I should relax. Everyone just likes her like I do. Stop worrying.*

When he was finished with his sandwich and soup he took his dishes back to the clean-up station and he too went to Pat's table. "Finished? Want me to take your dishes back?"

Pat was done and smiled at him. "Thank you. And I'll see you at two?"

George picked up her plate and bowl and smiled down at her. "Yes. I'll come get you," and he walked away smiling to himself.

Pat stood up and retrieved her *stupid apparatus* as she called it, and started her walk. *He is surely a nice old guy,* she thought and then on her slow way to her apartment she thought about the Ferry Lady, as the press was calling her, and decided now was a good time to call her old partner Gail from DHS. Things were certainly getting interesting here. Now if she could only walk properly again.

"Is that you? My God. I thought you were lost."

"Yep it's me and no I'm not lost, just stuck up here on an island by Seattle. How's things there?"

"Status quo. Some ups and some downs. How are you?"

"That's why I'm calling. I need a little help. First

I need some of my clothes sent here. Could you manage that?"

There was a silence then came the answer. "I just got a pen, tell me what you need."

Pat told her about the clothes she wanted and where to find them in the condo, and about the laptop. "The one Willy gave me is too old to do what I want, and I could use some info. Can you talk?"

Another silence. "No. Can I call you back or should you call me?"

They discussed a time for later that night using few words and some coded phrases. Pat then said, "I'll call you at the old number.

"Good. Later." And her friend hung up.

Pat was pleased to have made contact with Gail on her first try. She set her alarm clock to wake her at one-thirty in case she dropped off to sleep, then sat back in the recliner and closed her eyes. This leg needed rest and apparently so did she because she was asleep and snoring quietly in just a few minutes.

CHAPTER 17

Do you need a blanket for your legs?" George helped Pat get into the car and he'd put the walker in the back seat. "I have one in the trunk you could use."

"No this is just fine. The car's all warm and I'm happy."

George shut the car door without another word and went around to the driver's side, but as he opened the door and got in he said, "I have bottled water and a thermos of coffee too if we want it later."

Pat smiled at him. *Ever ready George,* she thought.

He drove out the driveway and turned left on Elm Avenue and then right onto Adams. When they go to the corner he stopped and pointed to the right. "That's Murph's Place. Have you heard about it?"

"Oh that's where the Tuesday Poker games are, huh?"

George nodded and he was happy to have a

subject to talk about. That seemed to be his biggest problem with small talk. Thinking of a subject but now he could just tell her Murph's story.

"Murph grew up here on the island, went to the University and then joined the Seattle Police Department. He did real good and became a detective then became a part of a group that used dogs to detect drugs. Several years ago he was on a case in a warehouse and got trapped. Both him and his dog got shot. The dog got retired and returned to be a stud at the place where they breed those police dogs in Maine, and Murph retired back to this island. Still has a bullet in his back that they say is inoperable so he just lives with it."

"My gosh. Isn't he in a lot of pain?" Pat knew first hand that being shot was painful and to still having the bullet in you body, well that must be bad.

"He says it only hurts sometimes."

Pat made a mental note to meet this guy. *Sometimes* was not really when it hurts, she was sure of that. While he was telling her about Murph they had just been sitting at the stop sign. Pat realized that the traffic surely wasn't heavy. Not a single car came up behind them.

Story finished, George turned left onto Willow Avenue and started telling her about the Haven Port Golf course they could see on their right. "They have Best Ball Tournaments and Tuesday's are for Ladies only until two. Nice little course with a few hills and ponds to contend with. Do you play golf?"

This was the most Pat had ever heard George talk. Maybe he was finally feeling comfortable with her. "Have played some but just when I think I get the hang of it I don't play for a long time and need to start all over."

"If you're feeling up to it when the weather calms down and you can walk better, maybe we could give it a try."

"Well, maybe I could go ride in the cart while you play the first nine or something. I wouldn't want to slow you down."

George liked the sound of that. "We could arrange that." To have her company for the couple of hours it took him to play nine holes sounded good to him. They continued their drive with George pointing out places of interest. "There's the Presbyterian Church," and as he turned west on Monroe Street he said, "... and then if you go back that way down Monroe you would see the schools."

Pat looked where he pointed but guessed the schools were a couple of blocks down. When she looked back they were on The Point; a thinner strip of land that trailed off of Haven Port like a wake following a boat. George stopped at the security gate and announced into the speaker who he was and that he was here to see the Nelson's. The gate keeper checked her list and in just a few seconds the gate opened and they drove trough. Now Pat could see that The Point was actually a big hill with the golf course on the top and houses and condo's cascading down the sides.

The houses at The Point were all expensive custom-builds, and the general consensus of the island was, ostentatious. Pillared entry ways and marble patios and heated driveways were just a few ways these people wasted their money.

The Nelson house was on the far end of The Point on the corner of Driver Boulevard and 3 Iron Street, one of the two one-ways on this spit. "This is a private course and you have to live at the Point to belong. Lot's of us have played here and it's a fun course because of the hills but it's by invitation only."

Pat looked at the men standing on the course waiting to tee off and she caught her breath. She recognized one of them. Someone from her past life and she thought, *Oh my God. How did Grant ever find this place?*

George was driving very slowly on this one-way street, as the ten mile an hour sign dictated, and he followed her gaze. "There's one guy I know in that group. Brad something. He works at the University satellite campus. Have you met him?"

"Is that the guy in the black jacket that's taking the tee now?"

"No, it's the guy in the tan jacket."

Pat nodded. That was Grant all right. Why would he be here and going under the name of Brad? She made a mental note to discuss this tonight with Gail.

At the corner George turned onto Driver Boulevard then into the driveway of the Nelson's house. "I'll go see if anyone's home," he said and got out of the car.

Pat watched him as he walked to the front door. His stride was long and firm, not like the walking pattern he had at St. Francis. This was the George of old. Very confident and in control of his world.

He was back in just a few minutes and opened the car door by Pat's side. "The place is empty but I have a key if you'd like to come in while I measure." She decided she would and George got her walker out of the back and placed it in front of her. Then he went back to the trunk and got a small tool box. Back at her side he said, "Ready? You'll like this house, it's something to see."

A beautiful parquet floor greeted them at the door and Pat could see it spread into the room on her left that held a glass dining room table and twelve low, swivel dining chairs all covered with the same red brocade. On the table was a long red brocade runner that matched the chairs and on top of that, a bouquet of white and red Carnations in a beautiful crystal vase. There must have been three dozen flowers in that large vessel. A dark rug of reds and blues was under the table and chairs, and tied it all together. And, as Pat stepped further into the entry hall, she could see a long buffet at the side of the dining room with five crystal candle holders lined up sporting white tapers.

On the right side of the entry was a room that was hidden by double doors that were shut. Straight ahead was the banister and stairway that George was working on.

"You can sit here on this bench if you want or if that's too hard, I can get a chair from..."

"This will be fine. From here I can watch you," said Pat.

He nodded and without another word, George opened his box and took out a soft cloth measuring tape and set about his work. He measured and marked in his notebook all the way from the circumference of the top of the post, then several other places down to where it was set into the base. It took him about twenty minutes. Pat watched as he worked his way from the front of the stairway to the last of the posts that were visible from this floor. Then he went up the stairs and was gone almost ten more minutes.

She spent her time looking at the painting on the short wall opposite her and at the display in the massive china closet on the far dining room wall.

The painting was an original oil done in the

style of Monet but using brighter, primary colors; a garden path with red and blue flowers, and a potting shed at the end of the path that was partially hidden by branches from a flowering tree. Very lovely. And in the china closet she could see goblets of crystal in several sizes and vases of both glass and china, and some red glass pieces. The china vases varied in size and color but were artfully placed among the other pieces. On the top was a display of four large platters that all looked hand painted. Pat wondered if an artist lived here.

George came down the stairs smiling. He was truly in his element now, measuring and planning for the new stairway pieces. "I'm finished for now."

Pat stood up and said, "Okay. This was interesting," and started towards the door.

Back in the car with the walker put away in the trunk along with his tool box she said, "What exactly are you doing to this stairway. It looks fine the way it is."

"The Nelson's just took a trip to Africa and they brought back some carved pieces they want to incorporate into the banister. I've already measured their pieces and now I know I need to make different and bigger support pieces." He stopped and looked at Pat. "I'm just going on and on, aren't I?"

"Well, I asked didn't I? Doesn't seem to be going on and on if I'm interested."

George smiled. Made sense to him. "Well, they brought back some extra wood too so I need to measure carefully so I can incorporate it into the existing supports since there isn't enough to completely redo the whole support system or the posts."

"I've seen some of the figures from Africa. Are

these in the shape of animals or people or plants?"

"Well these are heads of owls and cats and I think some dogs. All the same size but I think I'll draw it up first so that there are no mistakes of what they want and what I think they want." He turned to Pat. "Ready to go back?"

George seemed lost in thought about the drawings as he drove back down Driver Boulevard but when he turned left down 2 Iron Drive he said, "These streets along the golf course are all one-way so you'll get the view from the other side of this spit too."

Pat looked to see if the foursome was still on the course but if they were, they couldn't be seen from this vantage point, and she could only catch peeks of water between all the houses that marched along the south side of the street.

George went back into his planning mode and didn't speak again until they were almost back at St. Francis. "Did you want to stop at Murph's for a drink or cup of coffee?"

"Not this time. I'm ready again to put my leg up. This cast is so heavy to drag around. I think that's what makes me so tired."

"Well then maybe you'd like to go with me to Murphs on Tuesday. I think I heard you say you play Poker, don't you?"

"Yes, a little. Do they let just anyone play and do they play for money?"

"Well yes, anyone can play and the stakes are pretty high. Once I was a big winner and came home with five dollars." And then he chuckled.

Pat looked at him. This was the first time she'd really paid attention to him laughing and it made her smile. Such a big man for such a soft laugh.

CHAPTER 18

Dinner had been good. Tonight there had been choices, as in most nights. Pat had clam chowder, baked salmon, scalloped potatoes with lots of cheese and a Caesar salad.

Sister Nora had announced that the University had had a fishing derby a few weeks ago and Dr. Chu, Paul Engles, Larry Williams, and Robert Owens, who would be moving in after the New Year, had all donated their catch for tonight's dinner. Pat really liked the food here to the point that she seemed to be obsessing about it and thought again to check on the gym.

When she got back to her room she sat down at her computer and to her surprise had an email message:

```
Subject:   INFO
Date:      10:06:42 P.M.  PST
From:      SmoothTalker
```

```
To:          Dutyfree

Y>@4  u}i2n  *25mzr541  =5q
w75l#88i 8?84l m 17bv7 3&gGv
csaa3/i0Bwl,, xc)*^/@+%#]{;$
```

It looked like something that had succumbed to a virus and gotten scrambled but Pat knew the key. Every fourth letter was the real message and this was a phone number. 425-555-8817 and signed by Gail. The double comma meant the end of a message.

Pat wondered why her old partner Gail would send her an email when they would be talking on a secure line later but then realized this was a different number and it was a local area code.

Their agreed upon time for a call was at 11:00 pm so Pat would wait until then but this was very curious. A new number and a local area code? She decided it wasn't something she should speculate or even worry about. She'd find out soon enough but now it was leg up time because tonight was movie night at St. Francis and George said he was going, would she join him. They were showing a James Bond and she had agreed that sounded like a good movie. She always enjoyed all the Bond movies and wished that she'd had some of the gadgets he used in her own adventures.

George showed up at six-fifteen and knocked on the door. When Pat answered he said, "Want popcorn?"

Pat smiled to herself. Always a man of few words. "For the movie tonight?" she asked.

He blushed and said, "Yes. For the movie."

"That would be good. Shall I come with you to get it?"

"No. If you want I'll bring it to the meeting

room. You find a seat and I'll join you. Want a drink?"

Pat laughed. "Sure. A rum and Coke please."

Finally he offered a half-smile. "Well I can manage the Coke but the rum will take a little doing." He finally was loosening up and he added a quip of his own, "Or we could skip the movie and go to Murph's and have a drink."

"Well, after my exciting day I think a movie here would do me, but can I take a rain-check? Sometime I'd like to go out for a drink with you."

George broke out into one of his rare full smiles and abruptly turned and left.

She now knew him well enough to know that he would show up at the movie looking for her with popcorn in hand so she better get ready and go. She closed the door and went into the bedroom. As she entered she saw herself in the full length mirror. The baggy sweatpants and sweatshirt seemed to be her daily uniform and really she was too tired to change, but she did pick up the comb and swiped it thru her short curly hair, and dabbed on some pink lipstick. *A little frosting on this unkempt package*, she thought.

The movie was fun and exciting enough to keep Pat awake and George walked her back to her room afterwards. When they got to the door he said, "Tomorrow is that cocktail thing, isn't it?"

"Yes, in the late afternoon. Are you going?"

"Nope," he said and turned and walked away.

Pat unlocked her door thinking that even if he was a man of few words, he sure spoke volumes sometimes. Just that fact that that he knew she was going to the Estate for cocktails and dinner meant that he cared where she went. She hoped he wasn't unhappy about her going but then, why would he be?

It was only nine-forty-five and not time for the phone call yet, so, as was her habit before bedtime, Pat stripped off her clothes, pulled on the plastic bag that covered her cast and took a shower. Then, wrapped in a thick terry cloth robe that Sister Nora had found for her, she propped herself up in bed with the telephone handy and a book in her hand.

Since moving here she had taken to reading books from the St. Francis library. The one she was reading now was *Curious Incident of the Dog in the Night Time* by Mark Haddon and she'd just got settled in and found where she'd left off when the phone rang.

"Hello?"

"Hi Babe. It's me."

Pat hesitated only a second then said, "I thought I was supposed to call you at eleven."

"I got antsy. You know how I am. Can you talk? Is this line secure?"

"Just bought this cell phone today and you're on a new one too, right?"

"Yes and I guess that's as secure as we can get right now." Pat put down her book and swung her legs over the side of the bed. "I have just seen Grant. Did you know he was here?"

"No, but I'm not surprised. I've been tracking the Russian and he was in Seattle as late as last Friday so would Grant be far away? And before we get too deep into this, I just wanted to tell you that I'm here. I checked into the Mountain View Motel about an hour ago. Any chance we can get together tonight?"

Pat hesitated a minute. "Better be tomorrow. The office here is closed and it would cause an unnecessary stir to have a visitor. How about coming over around eight tomorrow for breakfast. The food here is good and then we can set a cover for you as my friend bringing me clothes."

"Good idea. I have a car so I'll be there at eight. See you then," and Gail disconnected.

Pat closed her cell phone and slipped it back into its case. As she swung her leg back into the bed she realized it had just been hours since she had talked to Gail and now she was here. Curious. But she was here, so now she had someone to do the leg work that she wanted to do. She picked up the book again but decided she was ready for sleep. And as she drifted off she thought about the Russian being here too and decided that that was the piece of the puzzle that made the Charlene's body being found even more interesting.

CHAPTER 19

Pat found Sister Nora in the office at seven-forty-five and explained about her friend, and asked if she could invite her for breakfast.

"Of course. This is your home and your friends are welcome. And since the Chu's are off traveling again you'll have plenty of room at your table. Just you and Natalie and your guest."

"Thank you Sister, and I'll just wait here for her if that's okay. Or maybe I'll wait outside in the sunshine. Would you mind opening the door for me?" Managing the walker and the heavy outside glass door was a little more than she could handle.

Sister Nora smiled and after Pat was outside she turned back to the typing she was doing on the computer.

The sun felt warm and the wind had stopped blowing. In just a few minutes Gail turned into the driveway and parked in the visitor space. She was out of the car almost before it was parked, hugging Pat and then she stepped back to look at her friend. "Sorry mess you've gotten yourself into, huh?"

Pat laughed. "I've finished the sorry stuff. Now I have things to do but no legs to do it with. I'm so glad you're here."

"Me too. Shall I bring in your things now?"

"Yes. Let's get that done then go to breakfast. You won't believe the food here. I was really surprised it was so un-institutional."

Gail gave her remote a click and with a beep the trunk of the car opened. In it were two boxes and a small suitcase. Pat looked at her friend. She was now a red head and it seemed as though she'd lost a few pounds but she was still the five-foot six-inch solid framed beauty she always was. The red hair complimented the dusting of freckles on her nose and the slight tan that showed on her bare legs was also very complimentary. She was wearing a short denim skort, the shorts and skirt combination that was so popular on golf courses and everywhere in Southern California. Her v-necked tee shirt was a bright green and so was the visor she wore. Everything about her screamed California Girl, except for the Birkenstock sandals. That screamed Seattle.

"Love your shoes."

Gail came back holding the suitcase and set it down by her feet. "I got these yesterday, on my way here from the air port. At a place in Everett. After you can wear shoes again, we'll get you some too. A lady I talked to on the plane once told me how wonderful they were so I thought I'd try them. She was so right."

"Let's take the suitcase in and then come back for the boxes. I walk so slow that breakfast will be over before we can get unloaded."

Gail smiled and closed the trunk of the car.

"Okay. Don't want to miss breakfast, do we."

Pat set the pace and the two women walked slowly to Pat's room. Gail washed her hands, and then they went to the dining room. They got in line and could smell the sausage and cinnamon rolls before they could be seen. Both women filled their plates with scrambled eggs, sausage links and two cinnamon rolls. They were just arriving at their table when Sister Nora walked by.

"Oh Sister, and you too Natalie, this is my friend Gail. She brought me some of my clothes. Gail, this is Sister Nora. She runs this place."

Gail set her tray down and offered her hand. As they shook she said, "It's a nice place you run. And the smell of the food is enough to entice me to move in here too."

"I'm happy you could visit." And turning to Pat she said, "Do I need to find a bed for your friend?"

Gail answered for her. "Oh, no Sister. I'm staying at a motel. But thanks for asking."

"It's my pleasure. You ladies have a good day." Sister Nora smiled and went to the next table.

As they sat down Natalie said, "I didn't know you were expecting a guest." She was a little put out. She thought maybe she was being left out.

"I didn't know she was coming until she called last night." Then to Gail she said, "Natalie was kind enough to take me under her wing and introduce me around when I first got here."

"Well it was the least I could do for a new person. But I'm sorry to inform you that I must leave. I've had my breakfast and I'm expected at the Estate at eleven." With this said she stood, picked up her tray and left.

"Okay. Except for Natalie, I think this is just too

good a place to lay-up. How did Willy find it?" Gail was looking around at the other tables and taking bites of the delicious food in-between questions.

"Natalie is a bit much but she's usually out somewhere. I think Bambi found this place. She wanted me far away from them as possible but still close enough so Willy could visit. I'll have to hand it to her, this is as good place as any to plant me until I can walk properly again." Pat took a bite of her cinnamon roll and chewed. "Mmmm, this is good, but by the time that happens I'll probably weigh three hundred pounds."

Gail took a bite of her roll too. "You're so right. This is great. Can you get out to the gym or do they even have a gym here in no-where land?"

"Dr. Pete is the doctor here and he says they do, and I can start going as soon as they take off this heavy cast, and that reminds me. He said we could do x-rays again this week. Wonder if it could be tomorrow and then I might just get a brace and use a cane or crutch instead of this stupid walker. I'll talk with him as soon as I can this morning."

They continued to eat and chat and as Gail was bringing their second cup of coffee back to the table, Sister Nora stopped her. "Do you have things that need to be brought from the car? If so, Stuart is here today and could help."

"Stuart?"

"Stuart's our handy man. He's here to do some finish work on our solarium upstairs but he does other things too. Shall I tell him to meet you out front in half an hour?"

Gail said, "Thanks Sister. That would be just about right." and Gail continued her trip back to Pat.

As she passed the table with Steve and Larry,

both men looked at her with appreciation. As she set the coffee down on the table she said, "Who are the old geezers at that table? I felt completely undressed by the time I got back here."

Pat looked and said, "Well, one is my date for a dinner party today and the other is just a letch. Do you want me to see if I can get you a date to go too? Did you bring cocktail type clothes with you?"

"Well I have a LBD and high heels. Will that do? And if you can't find me a date, don't worry. I'll use my time looking at the town."

Pat looked over at Steve and when she caught his eye she crooked her finger at him. He stood up and headed her way. When he got to the table he sat down.

"Steve this is my friend Gail and I'm wondering if it would be possible to find someone so she could go to the dinner thing with us. She's just arrived with some of my clothes and I'd so like her to join us."

Gail looked at Pat. She sure was being nicey-nice with this guy.

"I think Larry got an invite too. Let me check."

Steve moved back to his table and as the ladies watched Gail smiled. "Looks like I'm about to be fixed up. He's agreed."

Pat looked at her. "Were you reading their lips? When did you learn that?"

"A couple of years ago. Just another useful trick up my sleeve."

In less than two minutes he was back. "Yes he did get invited and yes he'd like to take your friend. He'll be right over to meet her and then we can set a time, but if you'll excuse me, I need to tell Paul and Mary of our changed plans."

Gail sat mute. She could hardly wait to ask questions and get more info about these guys and the date laid out for her, and she knew Pat would fill her in as soon as they were alone.

Both Steve and Larry came to the table and sat down and George was watching all this happen. He felt devastated. Looked like Pat was hooking up with Steve, and her friend with Larry, and if this was the way it was going to be, he was out. He picked up his coffee cup and headed for the smoking patio. He had some thinking to do.

After the introductions Larry started asking question. Where did she live? Was she retired? He assumed she was single but sort of moved around that topic until he could see she didn't have on a ring, then he said, "Glad you came by. I needed a lovely lady to take to tonight's soirée. It starts at five so we'll leave here about four-forty-five. That okay with everyone?"

It was and then Pat said, "We need to do a few things before the party. Will you excuse us?" and she got up and with the walker in place she said," See you guys later." Gail stood up too and together they walked as fast as the walker would allow towards the front of the building.

"Man oh man. Did I ever get lucky or what?" Steve was almost panting.

Larry just smiled. He hoped Gail was up to the adventure of going out with his friend.

Both men pick up their coffee cups and the trays the ladies left on the table and returned them to the proper spot, then stopped for a coffee refill on their way out to the patio. When George saw them come through the door he picked up his cup and left. He couldn't stand to be in a civil conversation with the man that stole Pat from him. As he walked back inside he deposited his cup in the RETURN area and decided he needed a walk. He went toward the front door and there was Pat and that woman coming in again, along with Stuart who was carrying two boxes.

"George. I'm so glad to see you. This is my friend Gail. She brought me some clothes to wear when I can get a more manageable cast."

"Hello George. I'm glad to meet you." Gail looked up at this man's face and could see the anguish in his eyes.

"Hello. I'm going for a walk," said George and moved past them and walked down the driveway.

Gail looked at Pat and Pat smiled. "He's a man of few words but so nice. I'll tell you about him when we get these things inside."

Stuart set the boxes in the bedroom as directed and was gone again after refusing a tip. "Part of my job to lift and tote."

Pat sat down and hefted her leg up as she settled into the recliner while Gail sat on the couch by her. "Okay, tell me everything."

The story of Pat's last few weeks started and in a little more than an hour of uninterrupted details she finished with, "...and so here I am recuperating at this wonderful place that I was prepared to hate, surrounded by nice people that I was prepared to distrust, and I'm even having a social life of sorts."

"Let's go back to this body they found. If it is Charlene, and we can be pretty sure it is, then she must have been back with the Russian's again. Or past tense I guess. Do you suspect Grant or the Russian could be involved?"

"Don't you? Too many coincidences not to be. I haven't seen Grant for all these years and he turns up here calling himself Brad. They say he works at the University of Washington at a satellite office here on the island and he studies earthquakes. Isn't that the same cover he used in 1999, in Germany?"

"Yes, and you say he's going under the name of Brad? Have you met him yet and does he recognize you?"

"No, I haven't met him so I don't know. I was a blond when he knew me and twenty years younger. He just might not know me but would he know you?"

"I don't think so. I was in the office during the Germany problem and you and I didn't hook up until early 2000. I think I'm clear. When I go back to the motel I'll do a little checking and maybe I can find out where Grant is supposed to be. And also, I'll check on the Russian. If he's still here too then we'll know we have something. I'm also going to report this to Samuel. We might need back-up or maybe they'll want to handle it from their position."

"Okay. I agree. I'm not really able bodied yet and probably couldn't help much."

Gail looked at her friend. "Take this as a vacation and then when you are back up and running we can decide what you want to do. Have they talked any more about you retiring completely?"

"Oh crap, yes. When I hit seventy they told me I had to retire from working with the FBI, but then that business came up with the Elderhostel Murder and I was relocated to California, and then there was the nursing home situation in New Jersey they put me on that, and that brings me up to now."

"Well hang in there. Of all the people I know you're the least likely to be voted as old."

Gail and Pat both laughed. It felt good to be back with a trusted friend.

"Let's unpack what I brought for you," said Gail as she stood up.

Pat got out of the chair and hobbled to the

bedroom to give directions.

The two women spent the next hour talking as Gail hung up and put into drawers the clothes from the boxes. When she bent to open the suitcase she said, "I also brought you a little present." She fished down among the folds and brought up a plastic bag and placed in Pat's hands. "Just a little glad-to-see-you gift."

Pat knew what it was before she unwrapped the package. Just what she needed. She laid the package on the bed and when she unfolded the soft flannel cloth she saw the small Kel-Tec 32 caliber gun. She was so grateful that Gail had recognized the need and fulfilled it so nicely. Although there seemed to be no immediate need for this kind of protection, she still felt better knowing she had it handy.

"Thank you. Now I feel better with what's going on, or rather what we think is going on."

Gail smiled. "I knew you would."

"And by the way, how did you get here so soon. I called you yesterday afternoon and you are here almost immediately. You said you were in West Seattle yesterday and..."

"Well I was in San Diego when we talked. That was around one, and then I got lucky with a plane to Seattle at three and so here I am."

"Did you get a hop with someone or commercial?"

"Just so happened that my friend that tests those fighter jets was about to go up and come here, so I got whisked to Seattle."

"And now you owe him what?"

"It's a she and she owed me so now we're even."

Pat stood up and hugged her best friend and, as she was thinking of her now, her savior.

They finished the unpacking and it was decided that Gail would come back at four-thirty for their cocktail party. After she left, Pat once again settled into her recliner with her foot up. It needed all the rest it could get before the big event tonight and she put her head back and tried to organize all the facts she knew into a pattern so she could understand what was going on with Charlene and how the Russian and Grant fit in.

CHAPTER 20

The Russian picked up his cell phone. He looked at the incoming number and made a face that was part anger and part disgust.

"Da?"

"Did you hear about the body?"

"Da. That stupid bitch never could get it right."

"Did she fall off the boat?"

"Da. Fishing boat not clean and still slippery from fish. Then it rained. When they get to place for dumping, she is already gone."

"Have they been dealt with?"

"Da."

"Good." And the caller closed up his phone.

The Russian looked around his room then made his decision. He picked up his jacket and started for the outside door, then hesitated as he checked the pockets. His knife was there and so was the Makarov 9mm hand gun. He added the cell phone to the inside jacket pocket. All the necessary tools of his trade. He left the room with a long stride, even for his short study legs. He had people to see and places to go. Maybe far away places to go.

CHAPTER 21

At four-thirty Pat was ready but Gail was still in front of the mirror.

"Do you think I should stay a red-head or go back to blond?"

"Which one makes you happiest?"

"Depends on which man I'm with."

Pat's laugh was almost a snort. "And who is it now?"

Gail turned and did a little model-like walk back toward Pat. Monsieur Frank. That Frenchman from Canada. He's been assigned to San Francisco and that's almost in my back yard."

Pat looked at her with raised eye brows and smiled. "Hmmmm," then stood up. "Well, are we ready?"

Larry was waiting when the ladies arrived at the front reception area and Steve was just pulling up in the car outside the front door.

They settled into the car and Steve stowed the

walker in the trunk and while they fastened their seatbelts, not one of them noticed a sad face watching them from inside. As they drove away, George turned and went back to his apartment. He seldom drank but tonight he thought he'd like a little Royal Crown on the rocks before dinner. Or maybe more than one.

The Estate looked like a party was happening even in this early dark time of year. The windows were glowing and the entry looked like a stage setting. Broad and deep marble stairs led up to the wide porch at the front door. At the moment it stood open and just inside they could hear and see Richard Reinhold III and his nephew Bruce greeting a tall couple.

"Murph. And Lisa too. Two of my most favorite people. It's been a long time." Richard and Murph were shaking hands, then Richard leaned over and kissed Lisa on both cheeks, European style.

Lisa smiled at him. They were almost the same height. Lisa was a tall, blond *with legs that went on forever* according to her admirers and those long legs helped her to stand five foot ten inches in her stocking feet. She was also a jogger and loved to ski so her weight was in good proportion to her height. Although the blond hair was by request, it had been blond for so long not one knew her real color, not even Lisa.

Michael Joseph Murphy, Murph to his friends, was always pleased when he was with Lisa and even more so when he saw that someone else liked her too. He was also tall, just a little over six foot two, and although he didn't much like to run, he did a few calisthenics every day, just the way they taught him in the military and then as a police officer in Seattle.

"Glad you could come. And of course you know Bruce."

"Sure do," replied Murph, and reached over to shake hands with him too.

Bruce was wearing the mummy like bandages over his face. It had been almost two years since his fiery car accident, and the scars were still a great source of discomfort for him so in public he wore this covering his Uncle had had constructed.

"Go on in. Cocktails are set up in the music room and we'll be in to join you soon," said J.P.

Murph and Lisa made their way into the house. The maid was standing by to take their coats and as they entered Murph spied Ken and headed in his direction.

After the handshakes and hellos, Ken said, "Good to see you. You've met my wife haven't you?"

Murph and Lisa both said yes and each shook her hand too.

Then Ken noticed the newcomers didn't have a drink yet so he motioned them toward the bar, and that situation was taken care of. He had a beer, Murph and Lisa ordered a glass of wine, and Ken's wife got a refill on her martini.

Back at the entrance Pat and Gail and their escorts were making their way up the stairs. As they drove into a parking place Pat made the announcement that she would not be using the walker tonight. She had a retractable cane all folded up in her coat pocket and once they were parked she opened the car door, and by the time Steve had made it around to her side, she had the cane opened and was standing beside it.

Gail was being helped from the back seat by Larry and she was laughing. "I should have known you were up to something by the way you've been walking around the apartment without the walker. You think you're pretty smart, don't you?"

Pat just smiled and nodded, then started toward the steps. She was doing pretty good too. It was slow but not as slow as using the walker and the other three moved with her. Larry stepped in to be near her back in case she lost her balance, and Gail hovered by her side. When they reached the top of the stairs Pat turned said, "Now you can stop being helicopters, okay?"

"They were all laughing as James Reinhold stepped out onto the porch.

"And I thought we were just having fun in here," he said and put out his hand to Pat and guided her inside the door.

CHAPTER 22

The Greyhound bus pulled into the Seattle terminal and T.J. Jackson was not happy to see it was starting to rain. It was just another thing that made him hate Seattle but his father said he had to finish the contract he'd signed. "We always honor our commitments," he said as he'd put his son on the bus yesterday.

Stepping onto the platform he made his way into the terminal to find the men's room. He needed a hit before he went to find a room and before he had to go back to the Ferry Personnel office. When T.J. showed up at home in Texas, his Father called to check on the job and was told that if T.J. showed up by tomorrow at seven AM, he could continue his employment and yes they understood he was young and made a bad decision to go home to Texas to get over his head injury, and they would give him a short medical leave. Now, that short leave of only two days was over, and here he was.

Back out on the street he hefted his duffle bag onto his shoulder and started out. He could walk to the place he'd stayed in before but after walking a block in the rain he started thinking about who lived there too, namely the Russian who had given him this major head throb. T.J. decided to check into another working-mans hotel he knew of that was by the bus depot. With any luck, he'd never see the Russian again.

But his luck was running out. He stepped through the door of the hotel and almost literally ran into the very man he saw in his dreams every night. The Russian's back was toward T.J. and he was talking quietly to three men. When T.J. realized who it was, he turned and left but it was too late. One of the men in the group recognized him and made a gesture.

The Russian turned and moved toward the door too and watched as T.J. ran down the street. *So. The little boy is back,* he thought. *Good. I can deal with him soon enough.* And he made that phlegmy sound that was his nasty laugh and pulled out his cell phone and dialed.

Brad looked at the incoming caller ID then spoke. "I have somewhere I have to be, what do you want?" He was in a foul mood. This deal with the Russian was starting to unravel and so was the Russian. He talked tough but lately seemed dependant on Brad for direction every step of the way. Was he getting old? And exactly why would he need to call again. They'd said all that Brad wanted to say last night. The Russian got his money and was supposed to disappear but here he was again.

"We got problem. That ferry boy is back."

"What kind of problem would that be?"

"He see me on fishing boat and maybe saw

woman. After he leave I think all is okay, but he back."

"So take care of it."

"Okay and what is in it for me?"

Now Brad understood. "Take care of it and then we will meet."

"Okay. Where is meeting?"

Brand lost it then. "Listen. Do what you need to do, then call me. Is that clear?"

"Da. I will call," and the phone went dead.

Brad closed his cell phone and put it in his coat pocket. He didn't like it when a plan got into trouble and that stupid ferry boat kid showing up again was a potential problem. He'd seen the Russian and possibly the woman, then to have the woman turn up after the ferry drug her across the bay. Brad didn't believe in coincidences, but here it was. If the Russian didn't get this handled today, Brad would, and also take care of the Russian problem that kept cropping up.

As he pulled up to the Estate entry he decided to park close to the gate so he could leave early if need be. He turned off the car and got out. He locked it with the automatic button on his key chain and heard the responding beep as he walked the last several yards to the lit up house. He could hear music coming from the open door and he could see James Reinhold in the foyer moving towards the side room.

Brad climbed the steps and stepped inside. "Evening James. Sounds like a party going on in there."

"Just so happens there is a party and I'm glad you could make it."

As they shook hands James said, "We're in the library having cocktails. What'll you have?"

"I can get a drink by myself. You seemed to be headed somewhere when I arrived."

"Okay. You see where the bar is and dinner will be served in a few minutes."

James walked toward the dining room and Brad walked across the foyer towards the library and the bar he could see on the far wall. He surveyed the room as he walked. He knew most of the people here and that made him relax a little. It was one of his rules of survival, know who's around you, but then he spotted Pat. She was older than he remembered. He smiled to himself. *Aren't we all older?* He was deciding if she would remember him or even recognize him and then she looked up and directly at him. There was no flicker of recognition and then she looked back to the man she was talking to, so Brad decided it was okay. After all he didn't look the same as their last meeting twenty years ago. Now he had brown hair and was athletic and when she'd known him he'd been bald with a paunch and wore glasses. But she hadn't seemed to change much except for her hair color, the lines around her eyes and of course the cast on her leg. He continued on to the bar and asked for a German beer.

"Sir, we have Henninger and Weltenberger both iced or just cool."

"I'll have a Weltenberger. Cool please." He was handed a long necked bottle and refused the glass that was offered. It was not icy cold like most American's prefer their beer but rather at a cool sixty degrees or so, like the Germans usually drank it; their equivalent of room temperature, which was not as warm as most Americans keep their homes. He took a small taste. It was good and he took another longer pull on the bottle and turned to survey the crowd again then moved toward a group on his left. He recognized the sheriff and decided that would be the best place to start being friendly. As he started toward that group he saw sweet Emily and the doctor from St. Francis and another guy and his wife that he remembered was a doctor on the island too. Emily smiled at him and he raised his beer in a salute. Next to them was a group with the sheriff and his wife and a tall blond that Brad didn't know but wanted to, and then he saw Murph and another couple he couldn't quite place. They were probably in their late sixties or early seventies but they didn't live at the St. Francis. Brad had seen them on the golf course but no name came to him. Probably didn't matter but he'd find out anyway before the night was over. A couple of feet away was another group that held Larry and Steve and Paul from the retirement home with three ladies. Brad knew the guys from the golf course, and there was Pat. And he wouldn't forget to find out the identity of other gals with them. Couldn't be too careful.

A tall young man appeared in the door and announced, "Dinner is served across the hall in the dining room," and the gathering started to move in that direction. Brad was one of the last people to enter and found his place card. He was seated next to Natalie Greene who was seated next to James. Across from him was the doctor he didn't know and his wife. Brad started to relax. This evening might just turn out to be free of problems. At least at this party.

As the guests settled into their chairs, several young men started pouring wine. Behind Brad a boy of around twenty said, "White or red wine sir."

Brad smiled. "I don't think I'll have wine tonight, thank you" and the boy moved to the woman beside him.

"Not drinking tonight or just not wine?"

Brad looked to his left. Natalie Greene, James' lady friend was speaking to him.

"Well I just got here and I sort of chugged my beer down so I think I'll not put wine on top of it right now."

Natalie pressed he napkin against her lips and said, "That may be a good idea."

He looked at her. What ever she meant by that was lost on him, but he didn't have to reply because the first course of soup was being served.

"Oh I like this," said the lady on his other side.

Brad turned to her and said, "It don't' think we've met. I'm Brad."

"Hello. I'm Phyllis Owens."

"Ahh, the sheriff's wife. So happy to meet you," said Brad.

"Oh yes. The sheriff's wife, or my children's mother, or my father's daughter. That's me."

Well, a little unrest here.

"Can I call you Phyllis or do you go by Phyll?"

She blushed slightly and smiled at him. "No one has called me that since we moved here. I think I'd like that. Yes, call me Phyll."

"Okay Phyll. What do you like to do in your spare time? Do you play golf?"

"Not well and I don't play Bridge either which seems to be the other pastime here on the island. I work part time in Seattle, three days a week. The rest of the time is spent just keeping things going at home. What do you do besides play golf? You do play golf, don't you?"

"Every chance I get."

Their conversation was interrupted at this point when James tapped his spoon on his water glass and stood up. "It has come to my attention that perhaps not everyone here knows everyone else so let's just go around the table and would each of you please identify yourself? I'll start. I'm James Pritchard and this is my party." There was polite laughter and then he looked at Natalie and she spoke next.

"I'm Natalie Greene. What else do you want us to say," she said and looked at James.

"I guess that's enough. Just so people will have a name to put to a face."

Next was Brad, "Brad here and I work at the U," then Phyllis grimaced and said, "I'm the wife of the sheriff". Ken said "I'm Ken and the sheriff", and then "I'm Mary and I live at St. Francis", and then "I'm Paul and live at St. Francis too with Mary." This brought laughs from everyone. Brad paid special attention when Gail introduced herself as Pat's friend from California, but decided she was not of concern to him, then came Larry. "I'm Larry. I play golf and live at St. Francis," and Bruce who was seated at the end of the table didn't speak but James said, "You all know my nephew, J.B." Steve was next and said "I'm Steve and play golf and hang out at Murph's and live at St. Francis," then Pat said, "I'm Pat just visiting St. Francis," and again Brad was intent on looking at her but she smiled when she said her name and didn't seem to notice his interest. Ed spoke for himself and Flo. "I'm Ed and this is Flo and we live on Front Street and play golf," and Dr. Curran said, "I'm called Curley by my friends and my wife teaches at the high school," and Dr. Pete said "I have an office at St. Francis," and while Emily spoke about working at St. Francis, Brad smiled at her. She gave him only a quick smile then turned to say something to Dr. Pete. Brad still thought she was beautiful and was a little sorry he wasn't her main interest but when they'd dated before she was married, he knew he'd become too intense and that scared her off. It was a problem he had with many women. He wanted things to progress faster than they did and that was one reason he was seldom part of a couple.

James stood again and said, "That was nice, thank you. Now please enjoy your dinner."

The soup plates were picked up by a waiter and behind him came another with a salad plate of baby spinach, mandarin oranges and blue cheese pieces. As the plate was set down the waiter said, "Dressings are on the table. Please help yourself."

Natalie picked up the small carafe of Raspberry Vinaigrette with olive oil and next to her Brad chose the Ranch dressing. When he finished he offered it to Phyll but she was already using the vinaigrette too.

Natalie was very persistent in getting Brad's attention for conversation and by the time the main course of Chicken Cordon Bleu was served on its bed of wild rice, Brad could hardly wait to escape. And all the while Natalie was interrogating Brad, trying to find out about his job and his social attachments, Phyllis was drinking wine as fast as it was poured. Ken was taking note but seemed to be resigned to the fact that this was the way it was now, and he almost ignored her as he spoke with Mary on his other side and sometimes he and Mary and Paul were all chatting while they ate, and Phyll drank.

As the waiters stood by the kitchen door, James rose once more and said, "I trust everyone is satisfied and finished eating?"

Murmurs of yes and oh-yes answered his question.

"All right then. Dessert will be served after our music presentation. Gentlemen, your convenience room it up the stairs and ladies your powder room is on this floor straight back from the entry. You will see the entrance easily. Now if everyone would like to be excused, we will gather again in the library in a few minutes."

The trek began toward the designated convenience rooms, as James called them, and the dinner portion of the evening was over.

Pat and Gail headed for the powder room but because of her slow pace there was a line when they arrived. Both Pat and Gail wanted to compare notes on Brad, but that would have to wait for a more private time.

Behind them was the sheriff's wife. Phyllis was swaying slightly and she looked very blurry in the eyes. "What's the hold up?" she asked but it came out "Waz the hol up?" She put one hand on the wall to steady herself and said, "Oh. Only a two seater, huh?" She seemed to think this was very funny and laughed loudly. By this time Natalie, Flo, and Emily came out and Pat started to enter with Gail right beside her when Phyll said, "Hey. How'd you break your leg? You that old lady that had the motorcycle accident?"

Pat decided enough was enough. She turned and took Gail's arm and said, "I guess I don't need to freshen up after all," and started her slow walk back to the library.

"What'd I say? Come on back and...." She didn't really get the full sentence out before her husband was beside her and had taken her elbow.

"What say we skip the music and go home?"

"I don' wanna go home yet." Phyllis was loudly making her wishes known.

"Yes you do," he said and with his hand on her elbow, the sheriff guided her to the front door where James was standing.

"We have coffee ready," James said.

"Well, thanks anyway. It was a lovely evening but my wife is tired from a long day in Seattle. We had a wonderful time."

"Yes, wonderful time. See ya later." Phyllis was being propelled out the door, down the steps and into the car. No one said a word about their abrupt departure but several people were shaking their heads. Poor unhappy Phyllis.

When everyone was settled into the arranged overstuffed chairs and couches, E. B. Simpson came into the room and joined James by the piano.

"It is my distinct pleasure to introduce my nephew Bruce this evening. If you are a fan of his you know him as E. B. Simpson, and tonight he will play some selections he picked out, then he will play favorites of yours. Bruce, the stage is yours."

Everyone clapped and Bruce sat down. His opening selections were from Phantom of the Opera, then on to several Broadway hit tunes, and then Mozart's Sonata #11. Then someone in the crowd called out, "Play some more Mozart," and he did. He didn't introduce the selections but no one expected him to. Last year he was on his way to Portland to do a concert when he was hit by a carload of drunken teenagers. His car caught fire and he was severely burned. Even after many operations his face was still disfigured and he always wore it swathed in a bandage and never spoke in public. Guests at the Pritchard Estate knew his history and so they just relaxed and listened to his playing, and loved every minute of it.

CHAPTER 23

Monday morning was busy on Haven Port Island. At the Mountain View Motel, Gail heard her cell phone ringing and stepped out the shower with her hair still in a lather. She looked at the Caller ID and knew who it was. "Yes," she answered.

"Are you good to talk?"

Gail was holding the phone between her shoulder and chin, trying to wrap the towel around her dripping hair. "Yes. What is it?"

The person on the other end of the phone was Samuel. He was Gail's contact at the Department of Home Security Office and when she was working, Pat's too. "How involved are you with the Ferry body?"

"Not. Just recognized her picture in the paper. Should we be involved?"

"Maybe. Do you know the Russian is in Seattle?" he asked.

"Yes and so is Grant. He lives here on this island and going by the name of Brad."

"We know that. Stand by. I'll let you know what's next." And the phone went dead.

And while Gail was hanging up, Pat was standing by the front door, waiting to be taken to where the x-ray machine was. She looked at her watch. "My appointment is at nine. How far are we going?"

Sister Nora was standing by her. They were waiting for Stuart to arrive with the St. Francis van. "Not far. I hope they can give you a lighter cast and I'm sure you would like that too."

Pat smiled. "That would certainly make life easier."

As Stu drove up Pat started her slow gait through the door and stepped into the covered walkway. Sister moved by her side and when they got to the van she said, "Take good care of Pat."

"Like always," Stu replied and helped Pat as she slowly made her way up the steps he'd placed by the van door.

Stu liked working here at St. Francis. The people were kind and friendly and he felt like he was helping. His wife liked it too because he no longer went to Alaska for all those long months of fishing. The overall money was less but at least he was home everyday to help with their children, all eight of them.

There was no talk on the short ten-minute drive from St. Francis to the Doctors Building. As they pulled into the parking lot Pat said, "Will you wait or do I need to call?"

"I'll be waiting for you when you're ready to leave," Stu said and got out of the van.

Pat opened her door and was sliding out but Stu was right there to offer a hand and then he got the walker and they slowly walked into the Doctor's

Clinic building.

At the reception desk Pat said, "I'm here to have an x-ray. Would you tell me where I need to go?"

"Oh sure. Are you Pat Olson?"

Pat nodded her head yes but before she could say anything the receptionist came around the desk and said, "Hi Stu. I'll take her in. Shouldn't be too long."

Stu took off his hat and said, "I'll be here," and he pulled a paperback book from his coat pocket and sat down.

Pat and the receptionist made their slow approach to a door beside the desk. "My name is Candy. I'll help you get settled in the examination room then Dr. Curran will be right in." She helped Pat as she struggled to step up, turn and sit down on the high table, and when Candy exited Pat couldn't help but think how young she was, or maybe it was only from her perspective. Pat shook her head and laughed to herself. *No that couldn't be it. I'm still young and age is just a number. I need to keep reminding myself of that.*

Dr. Curran came in the door wearing a smile. He stopped in front of Pat extending his hand. "Hello. I'm John Curran. We met at the Estate on Sunday. Let's get a look at this leg and see what needs to be done.

And at Murph's Place the back steps were being rebuilt and just down the street at the golf course Brad, aka Grant, was pacing and talking on his cell phone.

"No I don't' think so." And he listened. "I agree. Yes." He listened again then said, "I will take care of it. Yes, today." He folded his phone and put it in his inside coat pocket. *That stupid Russian. Now he's done it. It's like he's trying to make this whole deal blown up in our face.* And he was still fuming as he walked into Murph's.

Sitting at the bar were three men. All of them from St. Francis and they turned to look as Brad came in. *Stupid old men. Take a good look and see what it gets you.* "Coffee please and do you happen to have the newspaper for today?"

Murph picked up the coffee pot with one hand and a cup with the other. He walked down to the end of the bar where Brad sat and set the cup in front of him. "Seattle or local?"

"Which ever one will tell me how to understand this crazy world we live in. Last night on the news I heard there was another body found in the Puget Sound. Some kid. Do you know who he was?"

"Nothing in the paper about that but I heard that too. Seems like a rash of that sort of thing going on."

Brad took a drink of coffee and said, "Yeah. I've lived around this area for a few years and never heard of anyone falling into the Sound and now here we are with two people. I guess I was hoping they found out if they're connected."

Murph took a drink of his coffee too but was looking at Brad and thinking *What is it about his demeanor today that's different? He's wound pretty tight to just be curious.*

Steve and George and Larry were looking at him too. Even the air felt different when Brad came in. Sort of charged-up with his energy, or was it anger.

Brad put down his cup. "Well, I guess if they find anything they'll have it on the news tonight, huh?" He turned toward the other men who had been watching him and said, "Think it's going to warm up any?" Today a wind was blowing from the north and locals called it the Alaskan Breeze.

"Not soon. It's the Breeze Season." Steve's off hand comment brought a laugh from the other men. "Usually doesn't stop for a week when it gets started, and this is only a couple of days into it."

"Sometimes it lasts for more than a week." Larry picked up his cup and took a drink. Then, holding his cup out to be refilled he said, "Remember last Spring? Blew for a month straight it seemed, then on Easter it cleared up and was down right hot. I think it got up to seventy something that day."

George surprised everyone by adding, "Yep. I remember how hot it was in the chapel for Easter services. Very uncomfortable until they turned on the air conditioning."

"Used to be we only got this Alaskan Breeze if we were going to get snow. Now we seem to just get the wind." Steve held his cup up for a refill too.

Brad took another swallow of his coffee and stood up. He laid a dollar bill on the bar and said, "Gotta go." But as he left he was thinking *they can make conversation out of nothing. Hope I don't' ever get that senile* and he stalked out the door and back along the golf course to his car waiting in the parking lot. During this short walk he made a decision. The Russian was too much out of control. *Two bodies in the Sound? What was he thinking? Like it wouldn't be a suspicion that they were connected.* That made the Russian a problem. Dangerous to this whole venture that was almost finished, so the next step would be for Brad to take care of the problem, but he knew talking was not the solution. As he drove down the street toward the ferry dock he thought, *No time like the present.*

That afternoon, Gail and Pat were outside walking. They'd had lunch together and now that Pat was wearing a strapped brace and using a cane they were enjoying the sun and the walk even if the wind was a little cool.

"Didn't think I'd ever be able to do this again. What a treat."

"Well no matter how much you want to, this walk will only be up to the corner and back. Later we can go farther but not now. Remember what the doctor said."

"Yeah, yeah. But let's talk about what's going on."

"This is what I know." Gail held out her right hand and held up her index finger. "First we know that Grant is passing himself off as Brad. Second we know the Russian is in Seattle. Thirdly we know that the body..."

"Charlene." Pat filled in the name.

"Right. Charlene was working for us here in Seattle. Working on that terrorist importing thing, and she turned up dead. And we know she was connected to the Russian and maybe knew Grant."

"I'm thinking it's too much of a coincidence if she didn't."

"Me too."

They'd reached the end of the block and as they turned around they saw a car coming toward them. It slowed then stopped. Sheriff Owen stepped out and said, "Well, well. Both of you together. How lucky. Care to take a ride, ladies?" It didn't sound as much like an invitation as it did a command.

As they got into the back seat they looked at each other. Gail was wondering what was wrong now.

"Where we going? Did we break the law by walking too slow?"

Pat looked at her. Gail still had her strange sense of humor but laughing would be inappropriate right now.

"No, not too slow but out in the open. I'm taking you to my office to talk. No use giving info to the enemy if you don't need to."

Gail and Pat both got it at the same time. This is what Samuel always said and the sheriff must know him. "Okay. Take us to jail then." She smiled at Gail and Gail nodded yes, confirming Pat's unasked question about recognizing the phrase too.

The sheriff drove down Elm and around the block of schools, then into the underground parking under his office. As the ladies got out of the car Pat said, "Who knew you had a secret entrance to the jail. Use this often?"

Ken Owens laughed. "Well my secret's out. I use it quite a bit when it's raining."

He tapped in the security code and the doors opened. The three of them were smiling as they entered the elevator and ascended to the main floor and Ken's office, and as the doors opened the deputy was standing there with his gun pointed at the them.

"It's okay Ethan. It's just me."

Ethan visibly relaxed and put the gun back in the top open drawer of the desk, then assumed a position that looked like parade-rest. Hands behind his back, legs slightly spread and staring straight ahead.

"Going to be in the office for a while. Could you hold any calls I might get?"

"Yes sir," said Ethan snapping to attention and he almost saluted then caught himself and immediately sat down and stared at the phone. Probably willing it to ring.

"Good man, that deputy," said Ken as he showed the ladies into his office. Pat and Gail were both thinking *over-the-top, that deputy.*

Sheriff Ken Owen's office was sparsely furnished. It held file cabinets along one wall, a desk in the center facing the windowed wall that looked out at the squad room, and in front of the desk were two chairs. Under the windows was a small couch. Only a framed letter showing he was appointed sheriff filling in during the last sheriff's illness and another framed official looking certificate signed by the governor with his official appointment. No personal pictures on his desk or anywhere else in the room.

When they were seated Ken looked at Pat and said, "I hope this isn't too confusing. Samuel called. He told me about Gail and where you retired from, or are you really retired?"

"Well, until this leg is fixed I guess I am."

"Okay, I figured we could protect you from prying eyes and any information getting out in this way. That's why this meeting at my office."

He looked at Gail. "Just so you know the cover, late last night I took a call from you saying your car had been broken into. I was at home when the call came because I was on-call. Okay so far?"

Gail nodded assent. "Is my car okay now?"

"Yes. They just fowled up the lock of the trunk and my friend at the hardware store already replaced it for you. He did it as a favor and because he is on a contract to maintain the official cars. He asks no questions and keeps a quiet mouth. Besides, he's retired from the FBI."

Gail nodded again.

He sat back in his seat and took a card case from his pocket then showed them an ID card and picture. The picture was obviously taken several years ago and it didn't say he was sheriff. "I used to work with Samuel before I retired and came here. I knew of you Pat, but we never met. Gail and I have met but many years ago on that Homeless Scam in New Mexico."

Gail smiled. She did remember. "You look different when you're not in rags and smell like urine and booze."

"That was almost thirty years ago. I guess I clean up pretty good, huh?"

The ladies smiled.

Ken opened the file on his desk. "Samuel said you recognized the lady we found by the ferry, and now that we have that information of who she was, we think we know what she was doing, at least before this final episode."

"I knew she was paroled early. Was it to work on a project?" Pat was sitting at the edge of her armed chair with her leg extended to the side.

"Samuel said she was with the Russian because he is suspected of...."

The door opened and Ethan stepped into the office. "Sheriff Ken, I need to go to a fender bender on Elm. Can you cover the phone until Howard comes back?"

The sheriff looked at him and then sighed. "Where is Howard?"

Ethan started to blush. It moved from his neck steadily up his face until his forehead was almost a beacon. "He went to get donuts." Then he looked at the floor. "Sorry."

It was all the three people sitting in the office

could do to keep from laughing out loud. If it hadn't been so stereotypical for Ethan, the sheriff especially would have lost it.

"Okay. You go handle the traffic call and I'll man the phones. And we'll save you a donut."

This time Ethan did salute, made a three-quarter military turn and closed the door as he left.

"He really is rule-specific, isn't he?" said Pat.

Gail couldn't hold it in any longer. First she smiled, then chuckled then laughed out loud.

That made the other two give in and they all three were laughing as Deputy Howard came in the front door all smiles, that is until he saw the sheriff laughing in his office with two women he didn't know. He raised his hand in a recognition sign toward the sheriff and moved toward the coffee pot, donuts tucked under his arm. Now he could busy himself with making coffee and figure out if he was in trouble or what.

"What a fun office you run," said Pat.

"It is interesting at times but these are all good men. I can count on all of them to follow orders and to give their all. What more would you want?"

Both Pat and Gail nodded. Truely. What more could you want from any of your team.

The sheriff cleared his throat and smiled at the ladies. "Now, where were we? Did we talk about what we found in her shoe?

From here on the conversation included words like Lithium ion, and omni-directional microphones and GPS satellites and the density of non-volatile micro-chips and questions about DSP circuits, and pre-amplifiers. And a discussion of a power source.

"If we had her purse, I bet we'd find the satellite phone that could be the origin of the..." said Gail.

The sheriff looked at her and smiled. Nice to be working with these professionals again. "I talked to Samuel and he said there *was* a GPS and voice recorder in a phone and he's checking the data bank to see what is recorded there. This should help us identify any information she gathered, if there was something before she died." The sheriff sat back in his chair. "And so we're on hold until we get something else."

CHAPTER 24

George was still standing by the front door when Sister Nora saw him. Several minutes ago she'd seen him walk by her office toward the front door, and she knew why. Pat had gone out for her debut walk with her friend Gail almost an hour ago and still hadn't come back. Sister was a little worried too. Where could she have walked to on that still healing leg?

"Maybe they went to the mall for coffee or shopping?" she said as she walked up to where George was standing.

George turned toward her. He hadn't realized she was even nearby, but he said nothing.

"Don't worry. Her friend would call for help if it was needed, don't you think?"

George looked at Sister Nora. *Yes,* he thought. *She would call on that cell phone she carries in her pocket.* He knew he was showing his feelings but he was worried and didn't care. His Pat was out there somewhere and might be in danger but just as he was thinking this the sheriff's car drove up in front. George opened the door immediately to see what this was about and Sister Nora was close on his heels.

"Hello Sheriff. Any problem here?" she asked.

Ken smiled and said, "Not much. We beat them with a rubber hose and they came clean immediately."

George was helping Pat get out of the cars back seat. It was awkward for her. First came the leg then Pat scooted along the seat until she could get her other foot out and on the ground. Gail got out of the other side and was watching as George patiently and gently helped and guided the leg then the foot. Watching this and the way he was so tender with his actions made you know that there was no doubt in anyone's minds how he felt about this woman.

When Pat was upright and cane in hand, she reached over and patted George's arm. If he hadn't been so tall she might have kissed his cheek. "Thank you. You are truly a friend in need."

"Well, thanks for signing the papers Ms. Baker, and I'll see you ladies another time." The sheriff got back into the patrol car and left.

Both Sister Nora and George looked at Gail for an explanation.

"Last night when I got home from the dinner party, I went to my car and someone had tried to break into the trunk. I called the sheriff's office and he himself was on call. Well the upshot is that it got taken care of but I needed to sign the complaint and so when he saw us out walking he picked us up, took us to the station, I signed, and here we are."

"We were a little worried. An hour was a long time for Pat to be out walking on her first trip and…"

Pat looked at Sister Nora. "I'm so sorry. I didn't

even think of that or that someone might notice how long I was gone. I'm not used to checking in and out. I didn't think anyone even knew I was gone and I knew I'd be back soon. Again I'm sorry I worried you. I'll try not to do it again."

Gail looked at Pat. She had never heard her apologize for her actions before. Was this a new Pat emerging? "I'm sorry too," said. Gail. I should have known someone would see us leave."

"No problem and I certainly understand. I'm sorry about your car. Did you get it fixed yet?" The group was starting back into the building and Sister Nora was walking with Gail.

"Yes, the guy from the hardware store came by this morning."

George was walking beside Pat. "I'm sorry you were worried too," she said looking up at him.

"It's okay." George was smiling. His Pat was safe and she was sorry he'd been worried. She cared what he thought. He was a happy man.

"How about having a glass of juice with Gail and me. I'd like you to get to know her too. She's my best friend."

George smiled wider. "You bet." He opened the door and held it as the three women entered. Sister Nora stopped when they got to the office and the other three continued down the hall.

Pat and George opted for apple juice but Gail had coffee and two of the freshly baked chocolate cookies with white chocolate chips. "I'm making a pig of myself but these are wonderful. No wonder you like it here with all these goodies and the nice people."

"Want to come to dinner tonight? I heard it's pot roast with red potatoes."

"How could I turn down an invite like that?

What time?" Gail finished the last cookie on her plate and took another sip of coffee.

"I hope I get to start exercising again soon, or I'll start to look like a stuffed pig." Pat laughed and then she turned to George. "I need a favor."

"Yes?" said George with that puppy dog look in his eyes.

"Could you go tell Sister that I will have a guest for dinner tonight and save me a few steps looking for her?"

Without a word, and as usual, George just stood up and left.

"He is so dear but doesn't really get the hang of small talk yet." Pat watched as he went around the corner and out of sight.

"And he's in love with you, you know." Gail was smiling.

"I know and I like it. Funny huh, coming from me."

Gail stood up and collected the glasses, plate and her cup. "Not funny at all. I like him too." She walked over to the return table and set the dishes in the tub then came back to Pat who was standing by the table.

"Want me to walk you home?"

"If you want. I think I need to get this leg elevated for awhile. Come join me or come back at four-thirty and we'll have a cocktail in my room before dinner."

"I think I opt for cocktails at four-thirty. We probably need to talk about all that's going on but for now, I'll go with you as far as the hallway to the outside. You okay to go the rest of the way?"

"Yes. Stronger by the day and more sure of my footing by the minute." Pat smiled at her friend and started out at a considerably faster gait than the last months had allowed. "I'll probably be running by the end of the week."

Gail laughed. "Wouldn't surprise me a bit. See you later," and she went toward the front door.

George and Gail passed in the hallway. They said "See you later" almost together and then George found Pat on her slow walk to her apartment. "All set for dinner."

"Thank you. And Gail is coming at four-thirty to have a cocktail before we eat. Would you like to join us?"

George stopped walking so Pat did too.

"I was going to ask you to go with me to the golf course house this afternoon then stop at Murph's for a drink before dinner."

"That sounds better than a drink in my room. I need about an hour to put up my foot. Can we go then?"

"What about Gail?"

"I'll either tell her to join us at Murph's or to just come to dinner. She won't mind."

George was visibly thinking. He had hoped to have Pat to himself for a while but he liked Gail too and if she was there he figured he could just listen sometimes and not have to do much talking. "Ask her to join us there around three-thirty. We can leave here at two-thirty, I'll get my re-measuring done and then we can meet at Murph's. Or do you think we need to pick her up?"

"No, I think she would prefer to meet us. Thanks, George. See you at two-thirty," and she unlocked her apartment and went in.

George started back to his room but changed his mind and went out the patio door to the smoking room. He'd have a little pipe before his date. Then he stopped dead in his tracks. A date? Yes, it was a date. Their first real date. He went out the door to the smoking room smiling widely. For sure a happy man.

At two-thirty Pat came walking out her apartment door just as George rounded the corner. He was surprised but as she walked toward him he couldn't help but smile. To see her walking toward him and knowing she wanted to be with him was special.

"Ready for our trip?" Pat was smiling too.

"Yep." He put his hand under her elbow and they walked together toward the outside door where his car was waiting.

Emily was at the desk and saw them go out, and Sister Nora was upstairs in the solarium and saw them, and Dr. Pete was coming up the walk from his car and he saw them too. Two happy people in each other's company, and all three watchers approved.

CHAPTER 25

The weather for the last couple of days had been windy and cool but this afternoon the sun was shining bright enough to need sun glasses and the air felt warm. The ride out to The Point was short, and Pat realized again that going anywhere on this island was a short ride. The conversation was sparse, as Pat had come to expect, however as soon as they approached the locked gate of The Point and the guard recognized them and waved them through, George started to talk again. As much to himself as to Pat.

"Just have to verify that the newel post is exactly what I measured and that the top of the stairs has adequate room for the figure they want there. Then I'll re-measure the width of the set piece on the bottom and the top step, and at the bend of the set. Want them to be as close to the same as possible. At least in design."

Pat sat quietly listening to his voice. It was soft but full of self confidence, so unlike his normal demeanor. When he was talking about or working with wood he knew that he was an authority, and the sureness in his voice made his audience know it too.

As they passed the golf course Pat looked but did not see Grant or Brad, or whatever name he was going by, among the golfers. She wondered briefly where he was today. And what he was doing.

And what Grant aka Brad was doing was just getting off the ferry, back on Haven Port Island. He'd walked on the ferry this morning instead of taking his car, and in Seattle he'd walked to the Second Avenue Hotel where the Russian lived. It wasn't a long enough walk to calm him down. As he passed the Asian Pickle Restaurant, and passed by The Bagel Shoppe and then walked by the night club where the sidewalk was being hosed down because last nights over enthusiastic party-goers had lost their last few drinks there, his ire was continuing to build. *That stupid Russian is going to jeopardize everything.* His stride was long and purposeful and this twenty-minute walk to the Russian's hotel fueled his anger with each step. If you looked at him you would see a calm, maybe smiling, face but if you could see the eyes behind the sun glasses, you would see the venom roiling and it would make you happy not to be the subject of his displeasure.

The peeling paint around the window in the door to the Shipyard Hotel revealed that this building front may be brown now but in its past life it had been a dark dusty red, and at one time it had been forest green, and before that a very dark blue. Brad tried the door but it was locked so he rang the bell. A very tall, very large man with a Suma wrestler's body opened a door at the end of the first floor hall and looked at him, then made his waddling way toward the door but didn't open it. "What'd ya want?"

"Came to see a friend. A Russian guy by the name of..."

"He's not here. Moved out yesterday." And the man turned and waddled back toward the open apartment and slammed the door. Conversation over.

Grant stood there for a moment. His mind was full of swearing and chastising himself. *You know that's what he always does is run away. You should have known he would leave when you got mad.* He turned and walked back to the ferry. *Might as well go home.* As he was walking he opened his cell phone and dialed the Russian's number. No answer and he knew the phone was probably in some sewer by now. Grant aka Brad kept walking back toward the ferry dock then changed his mind and waved down a passing cab. "Harbor Island," he said as he got into the back seat. Don't know the address but I'll be able to find the right warehouse."

"You got it fellow," said the driver and flipped up the arm that set the charges rolling upward. There was lots of traffic for this time of day and the taxi driver said, "Sorry, ferry unloading" although that explained it, it didn't make the almost twenty-minute ride slow Grant's anger. As they drove down the off ramp from the West Seattle Freeway, Grant directed the taxi to stop on the north side of the street where the entrance to all the ship building and repair companies had their warehouses that stored the large freight containers that were waiting for the big cranes to load or unload them from the incoming freighters. The cab left and Grant waited for him to turn back onto the overhead street before he retraced the way they'd come then he turned to walk between two small warehouses to get to the one on the other side. No one answered when he knocked the code — two, pause, two, pause, three. This building was designed without windows, and Grant was really fuming now. That stupid Russian was probably in there laughing at him, but this wasn't over. He bent down and took his Sig P-232 from the holster in his boot and then punched in the security code for the door. When he heard the click of the lock he cautiously pushed open the door with his foot. There was no sound coming from the dark interior. Slowly he reached around the door and felt for the light switch he knew to be there. and with a click the whole area was visible including the Russian who stood in the far corner pointing a SSG-3000. The bigger rifle cousin of the gun held by Grant.

Surrounding the Russian were empty beer cans and McDonald's wrappers and a sleeping bags but all Grant could see was the gun pointing at him and he fired. The Russian was knocked back against the wall and slid to the floor. No longer a threat to anyone.

Grant put the gun back in his boot holster, turned off the light and then wiped the switch plate clean with his handkerchief. Then he wiped the door handle and the code number pad. He put his handkerchief back in his pocket but as he looked around to see if there was anyone paying attention to him, he thought, *This is not over. Not by a long shot.* As he started back toward the main street he was thinking it was time for him to disappear. There were starting to be too many people that knew him too well, and too many wrong moves by the Russian, and too many coincidences. People might start piecing things together. In his line of work, that could be very dangerous, and the fact that he recognized Pat, well it was only a matter to time before she recognized him too. He made plans as he walked down the street to where he knew there was a bus stop.

When the ferry landed back in Haven Port, he headed for his car in the ferry parking lot and as he was unlocking the door he noticed the deputy. Was his name Mitchell? He was walking down to the water by the dock. Grant watched as he stopped, took off his jacket and peered into the water by the piling. Then he laid it down on the much weathered stump and sat down. He took off one of his shoes and placed it on the piece of driftwood beside him, then he rolled up his pant leg, took off the sock and took one step into the water's edge. It was cold. Too cold for wading and Ethan Mitchell quickly reached down and pulled something from the water. Then, although he'd planned to keep looking around, he immediately changed his mind and quickly pulled his foot out of the water. He put his treasure in his shirt pocket, then sat down on the log. He used his sock to dry his foot then put his shoe back on.

Brad wondered what was going on and what he'd found. He watched as the final knot of the shoe was carefully tied and he started walking toward him. "Water's pretty cold, huh? What you looking for, buried treasure?"

Ethan looked up startled. "Just looking. Police business."

"Quite a mystery, isn't it? What have they found out so far?"

"You'll have to talk to the sheriff about that," said Ethan as he stood up and walked to his car. Ordinarily he would have stopped to regale this stranger with the tale of the woman's body and how he, Deputy Ethan Mitchell led the rescue, but not now. Just this morning the sheriff had talked to all the deputies at the roll call meeting, reminding them that details known by the sheriff's office were not to be discussed with anyone. And, that any new evidence that any of them found was to be brought directly to the sheriff, so Ethan decide to see if he could find anything new, but the water was just too cold for any extended looking. If he wanted to do this again he'd need special equipment to guard against thermal shock. He didn't really know what thermal shock meant but he'd read about it in a detective novel and knew it had to do with getting way too cold and he almost felt that way now. His one foot was *way too cold.*

Brad just stood there. *You'll have to ask the sheriff about that* he mimicked in his mind and stalked back to his car. *The whole world is full of jerks and smart alecks and I'm tired of them all.*

It was three o'clock when Brad returned to Murph's Place and parked in front. He had plans to make, but first a drink to calm him down.

The bar was busier than usual. He knew the three guys sitting at the bar, and two of the people sitting at a table by the juke box. At another table sat Pat and the other women he'd seen at the party. They were with that guy from St. Francis. George, if Brad remembered right and he knew he was right. He never forgot a face and seldom a name. He sat down at the bar, but away from the others. Conversation was not what he wanted. Just a drink. Actually, many drinks.

Murph was headed toward him with a cup and the coffee pot but Brad spoke up and said, "Today I need a drink. Black Label Jack Daniels on the rocks."

"Okay," said Murph and put down both the cup and coffee pot. "Special occasion or bad day?"

Brad was silent. His head was full of the plans to take him away from this hick town. It would be good. He needed to be where people minded their own business. Maybe back to Prague.

Murph set the drink down on a cocktail napkin and stood in front of Brad. "Anything I can do to help?"

Brad looked at him and then sighed. No use alienating this guy. "No just a bad morning."

Murph nodded. "Things always change and sometimes they get better."

Brad picked up the glass and took a long drink. Almost half the liquid. "And sometimes they get better," he repeated.

Gail was sitting facing the bar and was watching this exchange between Murph and Brad and Pat was also watching but only peripherally.

George was noticing the exchange at the bar too, but didn't really care. He was here with Pat and he was even enjoying Gail. And, he was smiling. More and more a usual state of affairs for him.

Brad finished his drink in one more gulp and stood up. Sitting here drinking wasn't going to help him. Now that his mind was made up, he smiled at Murph, put some money on the bar and left. Murph smiled back not knowing this was the last time he would see Brad.

Gail and Pat watched Brad/Grant walk out to the car and then paused. He took his cell phone out of his shirt pocket, spoke a few words, listened briefly, said a couple more words then put the phone away, got into the car and left.

Gail stood up and said to Pat, "I think I'll go to the ladies' room. Want to come?"

Pat was surprised. Then she saw the look on Gail's face and got up. "Sure. It's back here." To George she said, "Be right back."

Once in the two cubicle room, Gail said, "Grant is leaving. I read his lips. That phone call he got, he told someone he was leaving immediately. I think we should call the sheriff and Samuel."

And that's what they did. Pat called the sheriff and Gail called Samuel and things started to happen.

CHAPTER 26

While Pat and Gail were going to Murph's place, the sheriff's office was busy too. The sheriff looked up as Ethan came into the front office. The deputy was flushed and seemed excited. He laid his hat on the front desk and then made his way to the sheriff's office in three steps and knocked on the door. The sheriff watched all this happen and almost smiled at the careful protocol Ethan was following. *Always knock before entering the sheriff's office* was listed under Office Procedures and posted on the wall. It was number three on the list. Above that in position number one was *During office duty, place gun in drawer* and number two *If necessary to leave the office during office duty, notify the Sheriff (even at home)*. The next three on the list had to do with closing the office and coffee making. The sheriff found these reminders helpful for Ethan. He seemed to need more concrete methods of instruction and just using your common sense was not as easy for him as it was for others in this department.

"Come in. What's going on?"

"Sheriff, while inspecting the crime scene down by the dock I found something that might add to the case of the Ferry Lady." Ethan was standing at attention and making his report with eyes looking straight ahead and hands at his side.

"Come in and sit down. Let's discuss it."

Ethan moved into the office still in a stiff-at-attention mode. He sat down with back straight and knees together and ready to re-act to anything the sheriff said.

"What'd you find?"

Ethan held out the glasses to the Sheriff and said, "I found these down by the dock. Sort of hidden by a rock. When the sun got around to that side they sort of glinted. It was by the big rock that sticks half in the water and half out."

The Sheriff took the glasses and looked at them. They now had only one lens, then he put them down on the desk. "Good job Ethan. We'll have them tested. Thanks for looking and finding this. Would you make the notation in the daily log of what you found and the time, and so on, and stay here until I get back?"

"In the Ferry Lady case file?"

"No, not yet. We don't know if it's connected. Just the daily log."

Ethan stood up and in an almost military gait walked back to his desk then turned at a right angle and moved to the filing cabinet. He had a job to do.

The sheriff looked at the glasses again then put them into a glassine envelope and wrote the date on the top with the location it was found, and put them into his drawer. These didn't look like prescription glasses and they might mean something else so he'd just file it away with the can opener and the earring and the watch strap that Ethan had found in that location previously. These could live in the drawer until something came up to identify them. Now if he'd only found the other shoe or her purse, that would have been something.

The sheriff picked up his hat and closed his office door. "I'll be back as soon as I can but Deputy Howard will be in at four so you can leave then. Your shift will be finished." From past experience he knew that explicit instructions were best and as the elevator doors closed he could see Ethan standing at attention and saluting. He didn't say Aye Aye Captain but that was certainly implied.

The sheriff drove out of the underground garage and turned onto Willow Avenue then right on Polk Street to the Doctor's Building. In a few minutes he parked and walked into the reception area. "Doctor Curran still in his office?"

"Sure is Sheriff. I'll let him know you're coming."

Ken went to the elevator and up to the second floor. He saw Curley through the glass window in the door and he seemed to be talking to himself. Ken knocked lightly on the door and was motioned in.

"How long since you've had a check-up?" Ken was smiling.

"Not too long. Why do you ask?"

"Well when a fellow starts talking to himself I think it is time for concern."

Dr. Curran laughed. "Just doing a little dictating to the medical transcriptionist machine." And he chuckled again. "What brings you by?"

"Did the report come back from the Ferry Lady yet?"

"Nope, not yet. I called today and found out that a rush had been put on it. Should know something soon. Maybe tomorrow. Did you cause that hurry-up?"

"Sort of, but I can't talk about it. Let me know asap, okay? And I'll let you get back to that talking-to-yourself bit, but maybe you need to mention it to your doctor on the next visit, don't you think?"

Curly chuckled again. "Okay, I'll mention it to him but that will probably lead to a psych evaluation and that might be bad for me."

"Well, we all have problems. I'm sure you can handle this one by yourself but if you need help or some one to attest to the fact that you have always been a little squirrelly, let me know."

Curly laughed out loud this time. "Always nice to have friends ready to help."

Ken left and as he got into the squad car he pulled out his cell phone. He dialed and when he heard his wife's voice he said, "I'm on the way home. Need me to pick up anything?"

Her speech was a little blurred around the edge when she said, "No, but you have a fax, I heard it coming in."

"Okay, I'll be home in a few minutes." On the way he thought again how he wished he could figure out what problem Phyllis was trying to get over now. More and more she started 'just sipping a drink' in the afternoon but was blurry by the time he got home. At least the kids were all okay and living far enough away so they didn't have to be involved. Maybe that was the problem. Maybe she missed the kids and maybe he needed to take her for a visit. He'd talk to her about that.

He parked the car in the driveway and waved to

the kids playing kick-ball in the field next door. He liked living here on Haven Port and in this friendly neighborhood full of kids and activity, but if it wasn't good for Phyllis, then it wouldn't be good for him either.

The door was unlocked and he entered the house full of plans and hope. He'd talk to her right after he looked at the fax. His home office was upstairs in one of the unused bedrooms. As he went up the stairs he called out, "It's just me. Be right back down."

Phyllis's answer was unintelligible and came from the den where he could hear the television was on. That's where the liquor cabinet was too and that's where she spent most of her days.

It was only a one-page message and it was in code. The same code Samuel used in his message to Gail, and that Gail used in her note to Pat.

In his old FBI days of reading these coded missals, Ken could have just read it and understood but it had been long enough that he needed to get a pen and first circled every fourth letter then wrote it on the bottom of the fax.

```
Op[g<m&rv':a@!~n]%?t*%+/|)@req(u@#es":
<s!2%i;>?a+=0nax#   i*&lm.>?pee$o-
+&r=+qt?/<ixc^n(ujg  w*&T+@dexc&r"a&r>?*
i:?#scvxt 49^s 2~&a+=5rsq#r?>1e 9?1s#%(t
2@3s#%1a8&^n5*$<dr8:d>?re&ujtmi2a&%;i_)
>nv#2a#$irz5$r#n)i:?*v)&#i9j$n@+=g*/21
y#w8st]o<+*03u)T<cxor  j%dtt+as@1yo)?..
Sw+@mm[%M,,=4#n  "ncx0+=*8F6!2#40*ujn0  -
m2*t+!2@o*u(9d8%t^a?>zsy _+)*41
```

Grant/Russian importing terrorists. Arrest and retain. Arriving your town 1800 today. SMM

Ken looked at his watch. It was almost five o'clock, 1700 military time. He had an hour. As he folded the message and put it into this pocket the phone rang. "I've got it," he called down the stairs and he picked it up. "Hello..." but before he could identify himself Pat said, "Grant is leaving the island. Seems like he means to leave permanently. Gail is calling Samuel --- wait a minute." And he could hear them conferring then Pat said, "Samuel is on his way here. Be here around six but I don't' think we should wait. What do you think?"

"I agree. Where are you?"

"We're at Murph's Place and he was just outside getting into his car. That was about five minutes ago."

"I know where he lives so I'll go there. You better stay there or go home. I'll let you know what happens." And he hung up.

Pat closed her phone and both women started out of the lady's room. "We need to get back to St. Francis so George won't be involved," said Pat.

Gail smiled to herself. So Pat cared what happened to George, huh? Nice to hear there was real feeling between the two, or at least a start of real feelings and it couldn't happen to nicer people.

The women went back to the table and collected George. They got into their respective cars and Gail followed them back to St. Francis.

As they got out of the cars Pat said to George, "I need to go back to my apartment before dinner. See you later, okay?"

George just smiled and after he saw the ladies into the building he left them and went to his apartment having said nothing other than "Okay."

Gail and Pat hurried to Pat's room, at least as fast as Pat could hurry which was better than it had been for these last several months.

As she shut the door Gail started talking. "The sheriff is going to Grant's house, huh?   I wish we would be there too. Do you know where it is?"

"No. Some condo is all I know. Damn. I feel so useless just sitting here."

But while the ladies were talking, Sheriff Owens was pulling into the Cliffside Condos that were located off of Lincoln Street. He turned his patrol car around and parked it across the entrance driveway, headed down the way he'd come, and got out. He wasn't sure what Grant, aka Brad was driving but he remembered the car he'd once seen him in at the golf course. It was a light blue Ford Explorer and he could see one almost in front of him.

The sheriff had his gun in his hand as he walked toward the parking garage in front of the condo building and he heard footsteps on the stairs coming down to the cars so he started to move toward that sound.

CHAPTER 27

Brad knew the sheriff was there. In the condo he had an electronic surveillance with a video screen that showed any cars or people that were within ten yards of his parking spot, so, unfortunately, he knew the sheriff was here.

He cautiously came down the eight stairs and entered the covered parking area. Then he eased his way around his car, trying to keep on the back side and out of view. Then, when he reached the back of the car, he started to run. The dirt road in front of these condos led down to the bottom of the cliffs and to the open area by the marina.

The sheriff was startled by this sudden eruption of a person running out of the garage, but not so much that he didn't start running too.

Brad cut through a yard and took the stairs down to the beach and by the time the sheriff got the top of the stairs, Brad was already down the beach several yards.

The chase continued with the Sheriff gaining on Brad, then Brad ran through a group of people that were also walking the beach. When he got through this group he sprinted ahead.

Although the Sheriff had his gun in his hand, he couldn't risk firing it with so many innocents in-between him and his prey so the chase continued.

As they were running, a helicopter was landing at the marina which was located at the end of this spit, and when Brad ran out from behind the boat storage building, the pilot opened the side door. Brad reached the open door, dove in beside the pilot and before the door was fully closed, they were taking off.

When the Sheriff rounded the corner from behind the same building he took a shot, but Brad and the helicopter were too far out of reach.

The helicopter headed north but it wasn't really quick enough. The Sheriff read the numbers on the tail, and from past experience he knew it was an ALH. Maybe, just maybe this information would help find the helicopter, and maybe Brad and whoever the plane's owner was.

CHAPTER 28

The phone barely started to ring and Pat pushed the TALK button. "This is Pat," she answered. She knew by the incoming ID display that it was the Sheriff.

"The SOB got away. A helicopter came and got him before I could get close enough to shoot the bastard." The sheriff was mad at himself for not being better prepared and at least having a man on the beach.

"Did you get the numbers on the plane? Maybe we could trace it."

"Yeah I did."

"If you give them to me I'll have Samuel do the searching for us."

"Good idea and that would be faster than I could get the information. Ready?"

And Pat was. Pen in hand she wrote the information on the notebook she had open. The sheriff said he was on his way to St. Francis and they hung up. Pat quickly dialed Samuel's number and relayed the info. Now all they could do was wait.

The sheriff went back down the beach and back up the stairs to get to the condo and his car. He was still swearing at himself for not bringing someone with him. *Maybe he was getting too old for this job.* Then his FBI training kicked back in and he decided he needed to check inside the condo so he'd have that info to report at least.

When he got to his car he called his office.

"Sheriff's Office, Deputy Andrews speaking."

"Andy, do you know who owns the condo that the guy we had under surveillance was renting?"

"Sure. Mrs. Gray. She lives in Seattle now with her daughter."

"Do you think you could get me her number?"

"Well she's on the island this week for the Senior's Silver Golf Tournament. Her and her daughter are staying at the Mountain View Motel. Saw her yesterday. My Mom is playing in that tournament too."

The Sheriff smiled. Good to have a man like Andrews on the staff. He'd lived here all his life, except for his military service, and knew everyone. "I have a job for you. Is anyone in the office besides you?"

"Yes sir," and he started to go on but the Sheriff cut him off.

"Then you go find Mrs. Gray. Ask her if she has a key to that condo and either get it from her or bring her to St. Francis and meet me there. Can you do that?"

"Yes sir. Want me to do that now?"

"Yes. Now! And come meet me as soon as possible."

"Okay... I mean, yes sir." The phone went dead.

As he got into his car to head to the retirement home, Ken thought *I surely have dedicated men working for me but wish one of them had half a brain."*

CHAPTER 29

The sheriff parked in the Visitor space at St. Francis. As he walked into the building he almost ran into Dr. Pete.

"Well, who are you here to take away?" Dr. Pete was smiling.

"Here to see that new woman Pat Olson. She around?"

"Sure. I'll show you where her room is." He was dying to know what was up but knew Ken probably wouldn't tell him, but maybe Pat would later. They walked the short distance down the hall and Dr. Pete knocked on the door.

It was immediately opened by Gail. She smiled at the Sheriff and at Dr. Pete, and as the Sheriff walked in he said to Dr. Pete, "I'll explain all this to you later, okay?" and he shut the door, and left Dr. Pete outside.

These ladies were both excited and were ready to hear everything and maybe get into some action too, and as they listened, both were wishing they could have been part of the action at the condo.

For Pat, it had been a long time since something like this, that was in her old line of work, was in her life. Even when she worked for the FBI in an undercover assignment after she retired from the DHS, it was seldom exciting.

Gail on the other hand was doing some undercover for the CIA and chases were her bag. She had just recently been working on a case where the Father of two children was from Germany and was trying to steal the two boys from his American wife. Because this man was on the International Criminal list, the CIA became involved and there had been lots of action when Gail, acting as the Nanny for these boys, was involved in the actual abduction the father tried to pull off.

That was her latest gig almost two months ago, and she had been glad to have this distraction of Pat and her move so she could forget the last part or even all of the rest of this adventure. Now she felt needed even if she was on a sort of vacation.

The sheriff was giving them more details about the encounter and the helicopter when Pat's phone rang. It was Samuel. He had information about the helicopter. She put this conversation on the speaker phone so the others could hear too.

The plane was owned by a corporation that's ownership was well hidden, but Samuel's crew was searching. The plane was most recently housed in Portland but that lease ended at the end of last month and they were searching to find where it was parking now.

When they finished talking to Samuel and Pat was putting her phone back in her pocket, Ken said, "I need to go back to the Brad/Grant condo to look around. Do you ladies want to join me?"   And, of course they did.

As the ladies were getting into Ken's police car, the deputy drove up. Ken had a brief conversation with him, took the keys and got into his car. "Got the keys. Let's so explore."

Pat, Gail and the Sheriff arrived at the condo at almost 6:oopm. The days at this time of year were always short but because of the arriving storm, the dark clouds made it seem much later.

When they got to the condo, the sheriff again parked behind Grant's car after turning around, so his car was pointed down the driveway once again. He went first to get the doors unlocked as Pat and Gail hurried, or as hurried as Pat could, right behind him.

Pat sent Gail up ahead of her, and she was left, not exactly walking up the stairs but getting there. Eight steps up would take her a while to climb but she decided she wanted to see the inside of the condo more than she wanted to avoid the discomfort so she pushed herself. She could rest her leg and hip later.

By the time Pat got to the open door, Gail was busy in the upstairs loft and the Sheriff was in the bedroom.

At the entrance of the condo this what she saw: a stairway to the loft on the left, then the kitchen along that left side wall. To the right was a bedroom with a large walk-in closet and a bathroom. The north wall that was straight ahead of them held a window that almost took up the whole wall.   A very large TV was located in the corner to the right and next to the big window, and under it was a small cabinet. A very large black leather couch shaped in a U was sitting almost in the middle of the room facing the window.

There was a long table holding a lamp and

some decorative candles behind it. On the side of the room where the TV was mounted, sat a leather chair that matched the couch, and two high stools were at a small breakfast bar that ran partially in front of the kitchen, and that was all the furniture in this large room.

Pat said, "I'm worthless right now and I'm going to sit on this kitchen stool."

Ken called from the bedroom, "Okay. Take it easy."

In another ten minutes Gail came down the stairs and said in a voice loud enough for Ken to hear in the bedroom, "Nothing up there. Nothing in the bedside table, and nothing under the twin beds. I took the sheets off the beds and looked under the mattress and there was nothing there either. I don't think it was used. There were still even vacuum marks on the carpet."

Gail stopped at the bottom of the staircase and said, "Wow. What a view. Seattle on the right and those gorgeous mountains on the left." Then she looked at Pat and said, "I started in the loft since I could climb the stairs easily," and she smiled

"Guess I'll take the kitchen," said Pat and as she smiled as she got up from her stool then she stuck her tongue out at Gail. "Soon I'll be stair climbing too."

By this time Ken was finished in the bedroom and he came out into the main room. "I found a ferry schedule in the bedside table, and the bed has been slept in but nothings in the closet except a bag full of dirty clothes, which I'll take, and a tube of toothpaste half used. In the garbage were some used razor blades and a couple of tissues. Taking that too. In the closet he left a suit, the one I saw him in at the dinner the other night, and a tie and a pair of dress shoes.

Nothing else. He does travel light if that's all he had with him. When he was running he did have a backpack strapped on his back so he did take some things with him when he left."

Gail said, "Sheriff, did you hear my report about the loft?"

"Sure did. Thanks for being so thorough. Oh, and I looked under the mattress too."

Pat had been in the kitchen while Ken was reporting. "Well I found stuff in the kitchen. He evidently liked canned sardines, canned tuna and Spam, that sort of canned ham meat. I also found cheese in the refrigerator and three beers and a jar of olives. In the cupboard under the sink I found a fifth of gin and a fifth of vodka, both opened and about half-full. Also found a bottle of dry vermouth. In the overhead cupboard I found a box of soda crackers and a jar of peanut butter. Both of these were about two-thirds full. Nothing else. Cook top looked unused. Oven also. Pans all looked unused too. They were in the bottom drawer of the stove. But Gail, I couldn't look on top of the cupboards. Could you do that?"

Gail moved over across from the eating counter and literally jumped up on the counter. She was in a sitting position but moved her feet up under her and as she started to stand she opened the cupboard door by her shoulder and used the shelves to help her balance.

"Okay," said Ken. "Now this room." He was losing hope of finding anything of importance but he would check anyway. Part of his DNA almost.

Pat said, "I can help." She moved to the table behind the couch as Ken moved to the shelves in the table under the TV.

Gail reported, "Nothing above the cupboards."

Pat said, "Nothing in these two table drawers."

And Ken said, "Me too. Nothing, and as he crossed the room he said, "Well, I guess we are finished here. Thank you ladies for your help."

CHAPTER 30

Grant aka Brad, thanked the pilot as they were landing in West Seattle in a field not too far from the warehouse area. The thought crossed his mind that he should just get a sleeping bag and live here since he seemed to need to come here so often. He smiled as he also thought, *Not a good idea stupid.*

The helicopter took off and Brad reached for the phone in his jacket pocket. He called a taxi then called another number. When the phone was answered Brad said in Russian, "I am headed for the airport." He listened then just shut the phone and walked out to the road to wait for the cab. He knew he had some explaining to do but it would all be over soon. Maybe he would take a vacation then. Maybe they would let him.

CHAPTER 31

This condo trip was very interesting, but Pat was beginning to feel the extra effort she'd been putting out. Just as she reached the bottom step outside the condo, her phone rang and she answered. She listened then said, "Yes, I got that and thanks for the hurry-up job. I'll call you back after I know more here. Yes. Good-bye." She pushed the off button on the phone and turned to look at the Sheriff and Gail. "The helicopter was rented and the credit card used had been stolen so no help there. Description of the guy who rented it was too basic for an ID too. He was about 5'10", brown hair cut in a crewcut, brown leather jacket, jeans, no facial hair, his description matched his pilot's license and that matched the name on the credit card so it's all fake too."

"Pretty much what I expected," said Ken. "We didn't really find anything but it looks like he planned to leave and we might find something in the car. Hope it's not locked."

Back at the car in the covered parking, Ken tried the door on the driver's side and was very surprised it would open. After looking around the front seat and under it, then the back seat and under it, he went to the back and unfortunately the trunk was locked. "I'll have this towed and the trunk checked, but I doubt we'll find anything. Looks like he packed up, took stuff away, maybe to storage somewhere, and just came back for the night." He took a small kit from his inside jacket pocket and said, "I'll try to get some copies of fingerprints off the steering wheel. Do you ladies have any other ideas?"

Pat said, "I agree. He was leaving and you just caught him as he was executing the last of the plan."

Gail was nodding her head yes in agreement too. "Sort of his way. To just up and leave when a situation got uncomfortable."

Pat was now at the sheriff's car. *Boy was I ever a help*, she thought but she smiled and nodded as she got in the car. What she meant was she agreed with Ken. It was exciting and a very happy happenstance to be part of this Brad/Grant situation. It was almost like being back at her old Department of Homeland Security desk, but almost was the operative word. Although she was able to move now without that stupid walker and she used only a cane for balance, she knew she wouldn't be up to helping with much else on this search.

On their trip back to St. Francis Gail said, "Do we know yet how the 'ferry lady' as the papers are calling her, well, is she connected to him?"

Ken said, "This is all I know. The 'ferry lady' was named Charlene. Her last name changes with each job it seems. Pat recognized her from the newspaper picture. We know that Charlene was undercover for the FBI, and was working with the Russian that was also killed. His body was found in a garbage dumpster in West Seattle. From an eye witness report of a ferry worker, we know that Charlene was arguing with a man outside of a restaurant by the ferry dock and he hit her and she went down. We think that was the Russian. Then this witness saw that the man that hit her was directing two men to take her down the stairs to a boat. We also think we found that boat. It's registered to a Canadian guy we suspected of bringing in people illegally from Canada. It's a fishing boat and that night it was raining so the deck was probably slippery and Charlene's body slipped off the surface into the Puget Sound when the boat was heading out."

"Wow. You've found out a lot," said Gail, and both women were very interested in this news.

Ken smiled at the ladies. "I got really interested when this Brad/Grant showed up almost a year ago, and I remembered him from a case I worked regarding human trafficking. In that case he was a peripheral just like he was in this one, and we could never get anything on him but I had him on my radar."

"I for one am glad you were here and that I met you," said Pat.

"And I for one am glad you two knew each other before. Did you have a case together or what?" asked Gail and looked at Ken then Pat.

Pat said, "No, not really worked together but we were on the same team a couple of times like when I went undercover for the homeless murders in Phoenix, and then again for the importing of people into Texas for that underground mining company. I knew he existed but we never actually ran into each other. Did you know about me?" She was looking at Ken.

"Sort of. I knew we had you undercover for Phoenix and that you were in on the shoot-out and arrest in Texas but you're right, that's all I knew... oh, and I knew that we hired you after you retired from Homeland Security for both of those cases."

Pat and Gail looked at each other. "Don't we lead exciting lives?"

They'd arrived at the retirement home and both Pat and Gail got out of the car. All of them were wishing they'd caught Brad or Grant or whatever his name really was, but for now, they had done all they could and were done with this escapade.

George saw the ladies get out of the Sheriff's car but now that he knew Pat was safe he decided he might as well go get some dinner.

Dr. Peter also watched as the ladies walked in and Ken drove away. He was really, really curious but knew Ken would tell him what was going on when he could. And if Ken forgot, he'd sure as heck remind him.

CHAPTER 32

The airport bus pulled up to the parking lot by the hotel. It was almost eleven o'clock in the morning. A woman that had come in that bus was walking into the car garage and exclaiming loudly to an older gentleman beside her how happy she was that it was not raining.

A very tall, thin man also got out of that same bus transporter just behind her, and he too went immediately to the area where visitors of the hotel had parked their cars. He pulled out a key ring from his inside coat pocket and pushed a button. On the left side about fifty feet away, a car blinked its lights and made a slight chirping sound, and that's where he headed. He put his briefcase in the back seat and got behind the steering wheel. He had places to go and things to do, and he was in a hurry.

Last night he'd gotten the message that Samuel would be in the Seattle area and his instructions were to see that Samuel didn't make it back to his office.

As he pulled out of the garage he handed the attendant a credit card. The attendant did his thing with it and handed the card back. Now the tall man was free to go. Finally.

Flying from the east coast wasn't that eventful but after this job was done, he was going to take a vacation. First it was the Russian causing a problem, then Hans... and he tried to remember what name that stupid guy was using now. If he could get rid of Samuel and that stupid Hans, oh yes Brad, in the same trip, well it would be worth all the trouble of just getting here.

The tall man drove to the Seattle ferry dock and parked in line. He would have a twenty-minute wait until the next ferry to the island where these guys were, but he could use that time trying to track down his prey. He knew that Hans lived in a condo on the cliffs of this island called Haven Port. His plan was to take care of Hans then find the other guy. He also knew that the other guy, Samuel would be on the island already because he was supposed to have arrived yesterday. These stupid Americans had rules about checking in with the local office before they did what they came to do, so he knew approximately where that guy was too.

Samuel did arrive the night before but spent this day in Seattle at the DHS office, and as Ken picked him up from today's four-thirty ferry, Gail picked up Pat and they all met for dinner at Mickey's Restaurant that was just down the street from the ferry. The four of them sat in a booth at the back of the room, as far away from the live music as possible. They had things to talk about and clarify for each other.

They all ordered a beer and when it was in front of them Samuel started the conversation with, "Well, what have you kids been doing?"

Everyone laughed.

Pat said, "Well when I arrived on this island, so did Charlene. But you know all of that, don't you?"

He did.

Gail said, "I got involved because I brought stuff from Pat's condo for her to use while she was recuperating."

Samuel nodded.

And Ken said, "And I got involved because now this is my island and I'm supposed to."

Everyone smiled and nodded.

Samuel was happy to be here but was worried that some parts of this activity was not quite finished. Like where had Brad/Grant/Hans gone? And although he knew about the trafficking of foreign soldiers from Canada, he wasn't sure that Ken or the ladies knew of this terrorist activity.

The waiter came to their table and asked if they were ready to order. Samuel looked at Ken and said, "What do you recommend?"

"The hamburgers here are great. I like the Blue Cheese Bacon Combo. Comes with coleslaw and fries."

Everyone at the table decided that sounded good and the waiter went away without even writing it down.

While they were ordering, the tall, thin man came in and sat at the bar. He was thinking, *What luck. Everyone together except Hans.* He couldn't hear what they were discussing but it didn't matter. Now he could just wait for an opportunity to carry out this part of his plan.

Because of their professions and past experiences, both Ken and Samuel saw the tall man come in but didn't register any recognition. In fact, all the people at this table saw him and dismissed him in their minds as not important.

Samuel said, "How about if I ask the questions and you all fill me in? Would that work?"
They were all nodding their heads yes, so he started.

"We know when Brad/Hans left here and the Seattle area but we lost track of him. When did he first come to this island? Do you know?"

Ken spoke up. "Brad, as he called himself here, showed up around a year ago. Don't know the exact date but he told everyone that wanted to know that he worked at the University of Washington Satellite Campus here on the island, and had something to do with earthquakes. About three months ago I checked and found out it wasn't true but there didn't seem to be any reason to question where he did work or why he lied. However, I did have him on my radar just because he seemed to be so interested in being friends with everyone and fitting in. I marked it up as my just having unusual radar." All three of the others understood this radar thing.

Samuel looked at Pat. "How did you get involved? Was it only because you recognized Charlene from the news picture? And how do you happen to be here anyway?"

Pat filled him in on her motorcycle accident, how she arrived the same day Charlene did, and how she'd finally contacted his office for information about Charlene.

Gail was next. "You said you were here because of Pat. Is that all?"

Gail nodded first then said, "Because of Pat yes, and I stayed because of the excitement."

"Now Ken," said Samuel. "Is there any more details you think I should hear about?

Ken smiled. "I think we've filled you in on everything we know, which doesn't seem to be very much and I sure would like to hear the rest of the story."

Now Samuel smiled. "Okay. Here is as much as I can tell you. Brad/Grant/Hans is an operative for several foreign countries. Among them are Russia and Iraq. Between him and the Russian... you know who he was right?"

None of them knew anything about the Russian so Samuel continued.

"The Russian, as he is called because no one knows his name, used Charlene as a contact here in the US. She in turn had contacts to some of the underground workers that organized and imported would-be terrorists from all over the world, and she also worked for us. They imported people who would come through Canada, like the ones that arrived on the fishing boat that was owned partially by the Russian, and then taken to areas around the States so they could integrate into the society and be ready to strike when told to. Brad was one of the recruiters for these terrorists and sort of the head of a faction that got them to Canada, then to the US. That's one of the reasons he traveled so much and used the cover of studying earthquakes because they seem to happen all the time and all over the place."

Samuel and his audience of three were so engrossed in the story they were all surprised when the waiter started putting plates down in front of them.

"Need another round of beers?" asked thee waiter as he put down the last plate.

Of course they did and then spent the next hour eating, asking questions and generally being happy that they now knew the whole story, or as much as was necessary, to piece together all the events of this last few weeks.

It was almost nine o'clock when Samuel looked at his watch and said, "Anyone know when the next ferry gets here?" Ken did and they decided if they left now Samuel could be on it when it left at nine-thirty.

Since Samuel had already paid, "My treat to be with such great people", they all went out to the parking area. Samuel got into the front seat of Ken's car, and Gail's car was parked behind him. They all noticed the tall man left too, but again it didn't seem very important.

Ken took Samuel to the ferry that was just arriving and he got out of the car and walked onto the boat. He would call the car and driver he'd previously arranged for and have them waiting in Seattle at the ferry dock to take him to his waiting plane, and promised to update all of them if he got more information.

Ken had already made a date with the ladies to meet in the morning for coffee to discuss how this event had ended so he headed for home.

The tall thin man pulled out behind Ken's car to the ferry, but decided this was not the right time to take care of Samuel, and what he really wanted to do was find Hans, but he decided it was time to change vehicles. He drove down the first street he came to and saw a pick-up truck parked at the curb. He left his car parked behind it, went to the truck and got in. Didn't take but a few seconds for him to manipulate the wires, start it up, and pull away.

Ken was extremely happy with how this event concluded but he did take note of the pick-up truck that pulled in behind him when he turned the corner by the ferry. He thought he recognized the truck as belonging to the guy that hung out at Murph's sometimes, and sometimes at Micky's. Although his mind was still digesting everything Samuel had told them, he tried but couldn't see the driver clearly so he made a mental note to try to find out who drove this particular truck. It was missing a license plate in the front. The plate holder was there but no plate.

Just before Ken got to his driveway the tall, thin man's cell phone started to chirp. This was his notice that a phone call was waiting for him to answer. He pulled over, dug the phone out of his inside coat pocket and answered. "Da."

The caller spoke a few sentences then hung up and so did the tall man. What he'd heard made him very angry. Now he knew that Hans had reported in and was on his way to headquarters, but no one had deemed it necessary to inform the tall man he wasn't here on the island anymore. Some heads would roll over this snafu and he meant literally. The tall man pulled back out into the street but just drove past Ken's house and back towards the ferry with plans forming and maybe he could still get on the ferry they'd seen.

As Ken started into the house he noticed the fast acceleration of the pickup when it squealed away from the curb and drove by. He wondered what that was about and noted the license number on the back of the pickup. Again he didn't think it was really important and it could wait until he got to the office tomorrow. And as the truck drove by Ken could see the very tall person driving and he recognized him as the guy from the bar. Something else to check out tomorrow.